Eye Contact

Eye Contact

Cameron Liang

Published internationally by Cam Dusting 2025

ISBN: 978-0994513052

Chapter 1

I smiled at the golden statue. I forgot its name, but I always kind of liked it.

It was Saturday afternoon. I'd passed time in Central Park, but the air got cold. I remember hearing something about having to feel cold in order to be beautiful. I wasn't interested in that, and the breeze in Central Park was icy. So, I turned away from the golden statue, and made my way toward Park Avenue.

Someone grabbed his face outside Celine. I looked—he was elderly and covered his eyes, making a silly face at me. I giggled, distracted from the bags in the window. The man said something I didn't understand. I shook my head, laughing. The man laughed, too.

Then I was in the winter sun on Park Avenue. Wow, I loved Park. I crossed to the middle, bending to stroke my fingertips through the soft, red begonias in the flowerbed. The breeze wasn't as cold here in the street. I took a right. I didn't know where I was headed. Yet I knew where I was going.

Car horns blared. Voices rang out. Dogwalkers, families, and people like me. All sorts. They seemed happy, though it might have been my imagination.

I remembered Monday mornings. The drifters, the trudgers. Everyone. The City like machinery. Gray and cold. The people like robots. Never able to talk to one another. Never able to say: 'Hi.' And I was just another one of those robots! Lost people, fulfilled people. We were all the same, yet we weren't allowed to say: 'Hi.' The City was like clockwork. We were suit-dressed components of an engine. The engine was capitalism. All the same people, but all just lonely. You'd think that if everyone was lonely, then, well, no one would be lonely. You'd think that if you worked for a corporation, you'd cease to be an individual. Would that be a bad thing? Or a good thing?

Anyway, that was weekdays. Now it was the weekend! Maybe these people really were happy. Three moms with three strollers approached. The mom with the gorgeous earrings veered to her left, and I strolled right on through.

"Thank you," I said.

She smiled without looking in my eyes.

I jaywalked 56th Street. Ahead were the skyscrapers I'd never stop loving. Didn't matter what they meant.

The blinding sun refracted off the glass skyscrapers to my left. I reached into my Zara purse and fished out my shades. I slipped them on.

I passed Ferrari, I passed Chase Bank. Trying not to step in melted snow, I'd ambled all afternoon. But subtly, I picked up my pace.

I never use headphones when I walk. But sometimes I imagine the sounds of the streets are music. I danced a little!

Whenever I crossed the road, I gazed into the depths of the street. It made me feel good.

Here was someone. A handsome darker man. I smiled, trying not to be too obvious. But I might as well have been a lamppost. He didn't bat an eyelid. I did catch the scent of his cologne, though. Mm.

Oo, a lady. Older than me, taller than me. She was stunning. I shivered. I didn't know if it was because of the wind or because of her. Either way, the older woman walked right past me. Was I invisible?

I sighed, I felt sad. But on the other side of Park was the Seagram Building, with its black glass and its luminescent fountains. It was perfect timing, and my heart lifted again. The black skyscraper had been there since 1958. I didn't know about the American flag, but sure, why not?

Some more American flags fluttered over my head. Air tickled through my hair, a beautiful feeling. There was a church on the other side of the road. The ITT Building on my side. Now I passed the Colgate-Palmolive headquarters. Talk about money. But it was the weekend, it was my time to not think about any of that.

"Rachael!"

One of my colleagues waved from the depths of 49th Street.

"Hi James!"

I walked a little faster, passing more enormous black skyscrapers. Didn't want him to get any ideas. Here was a street-side newsrack. I smelled someone's food. I got hungry. And I got closer.

I looked for infinity. I never knew where to find it. All I knew was that soon, I would take off my sunglasses.

But not yet! I sauntered past some construction, I passed through the Helmsley Building walkway. Into the Metlife Building, through the revolving door, up the escalator. Every time, Grand Central Station made me say, 'Wow!' I ducked in and out between commuters. They'd knock you down if you weren't careful. They were barely visible.

So, I took off my shades.

Chapter 2

By the time I emerged from Grand Central Station, it was still kind of bright. I took a right, weaving in and out between passers-by. A nonbinary person stood in Vanderbilt Avenue. They looked good, they smelled good. I looked straight at them, but they didn't look up from their iPhone. Yet again, I was unable to get this person's attention.

So I tried making eye contact with the old man shuffling toward me. I smiled cautiously at him. He focused on his steps, head down, occasionally glancing abruptly to his left, snapping his head back down again. I smiled at him harder. He walked right past.

What was wrong with me?

Two little South Asian girls. Maybe ten and 12. Surely they would notice me. I slowed down a little bit.

"Actually, I prefer Dad."

"You're not supposed to choose!"

They were already gone.

I crossed Madison. I danced a little bit—maybe if I weirded people out, they would notice me? Some guy frowned at me, around my age. My eyes moved in his direction, but he frowned at my boots. Was I a bad dancer? Or was Celtic & Co. unsatisfactory?

I wondered if I was transparent. You just weren't supposed to make eye contact in this City. You weren't allowed to smile at strangers! Trying to convince myself that these were human beings meant I was odd. Someone shot down 42nd Street on one of those electric unicycles. Several heads turned. Someone whooped. Clearly, I needed to buy one of those things! But how would I ever learn to ride it?

I liked the 42nd Street Library, but its exterior always kind of annoyed me. Now I walked under that beautiful smooth skyscraper that said "GRACE." I stole a glance at Bryant Park. Colored bumper cars danced across the ice rink. Bank of America ads watched over innocent children. I looked back at the street, my happy place.

The ironic thing was that my real happy place overflowed with advertisements. And I was just about there. How was it that one of the City's best libraries annoyed me, yet the place with more ads than a small country filled me with joy?

You have to know where I went. I told you I knew where I was going.

I knew that the Black couple passing me were New Yorkers. I knew because they were leaving Times Square. I think I'm the only New Yorker who actually likes the place.

Anyway, neither of them looked into my eyes. Why should they?

The tourists up ahead didn't look at me either. They were too busy staring at the giant screen over the H&M entranceway. To entertain myself, I stared at them. Hard. But it didn't make a difference.

This made sense. Times Square contained countless sights more interesting than me. After all, I was just another person. I glided up into the hourglass. I swerved around a cluster of East Asians taking photos with expensive cameras. I had no idea what they said, though I wanted to. They definitely didn't notice me.

I twirled. A homeless man looked over, and I fired my eyes at his, slipping 20 dollars from my purse. The man managed to grab the note without acknowledging me! I made a sad face, and twirled again.

"Watch it!" an American woman exclaimed, stepping back.

"Oh, sorry!" I laughed, twirling.

She didn't laugh. She glared, but by the time I looked back, she shook her head with her husband.

Two cops stood outside the station. I needed attention!

"Hi."

One cop walked off.

The other just nodded.

I couldn't believe it! What was with these people? I watched as the first cop leaned in to hear the shirtless man who'd beckoned him. Obviously, the topic was important!

There were people everywhere. Once upon a time, only the Lenni Lenape people had been here. As far as I knew, Times Square would always belong to the Lenape. They had spoken Munsee and had lived among the sweetgums that had thrived here. Those people had never left.

Yet now there were bright LED spectaculars and flashing lights and multicolored billboards. There were little red tables and a whole lot of concrete and steel. There was loud music and wild traffic and voices. There were the scents of hot dogs and rice, of grease and sweat, of sewage and grass. And there were people.

Everywhere.

They stared at their smartphones. They stared at all of the lights. They sang and they danced. They backflipped and crowds cheered. They burst out of restaurants and they slept on the sidewalks. They zoomed around in vehicles I could barely name. I knew none of these people, yet I knew all of these people. I knew that very few were locals.

All sorts of people!

But even on Saturday evening, these people were robots. I liked to think people were only robots on weekdays. I liked to think they became humans again on weekends. But Times Square was a factory! I would always love Times Square. But why would no one look at me?

Chapter 3

Brilliantly, the sun fell. It was the weekend, why were these people so uptight? They were tourists. Even in America, even on a Saturday evening, everyone felt the need to conform to social boundaries. Where were their hearts? They couldn't even say: 'Hi.' Not even when I said it first.

They were too busy staring at Instagram advertisements. At McDonalds billboards. At TikTok on their iPhones. At Hulu trailers on enormous televisions. At American Eagle ads for brand-new winter outfits. I caught myself staring at the Lilly logo. Did I need to buy medicine?

The whole thing was a business. The Times Square Alliance received funding from the City of New York, but was officially a private not-for-profit organization. Every screen had a name and every corporation paid another corporation to advertise here. And the machine *worked*. The people consumed.

I love capitalism. That doesn't mean I don't think it's disgusting.

Disgusting—yet beautiful. The Spotify logo flashed in my periphery. Then I saw the little Twitter bird. I would never stop calling it Twitter.

Times Square was beautiful—but no one looked at me. Not the giant people on the screens, and not the robots who were supposedly humans. I sauntered through the factory. No one noticed me.

What if I didn't exist?

And then—*bang!*—eye contact! I smiled in disbelief. The woman with the head covering smiled back!

She was already gone. Yet this wonderful woman was the only flash of bright color in the entirely gray machine that was the chaos of the City. Suddenly, *I existed*.

It was self-realization.

I was real!

I didn't even notice my smile. Yet it made several people passing the red staircase connect eyes with me. One by one, the father... and the daughter... and the son... and the mother... all smiled!

I giggled.

Some dude gave me a yellow business card. I accepted it, feigning heartfelt gratitude. It didn't matter whether he advertised a restaurant, or his private services, or just some unknown joke. Since I never littered, I slipped the card in a trash can.

It was a collective epiphany. Now that *I* knew I existed, *everyone else* knew I existed! They all looked at me. They were not robots after all. They were humans! Eye contact with a suit-clad Middle Eastern man. Eye contact with his partner. Eye contact with a Latin American woman. Eye contact with each of her friends. Eye contact with Minnie

Mouse in her costume. Eye contact with a white family. Eye contact with a couple in wheelchairs. Glancing into a shop window, illuminated by the sunset: eye contact with myself.

I skipped in front of the red staircase. I twirled. Eyes were on me. Faces smiled. I smiled!

I was infinitely happy, and I did not understand why.

I danced! Someone laughed, and we connected eyes. It was a middle-aged gentleman, shaking his head. He thought I was ridiculous. They all did. I didn't mind.

I was so happy. Unreasonably happy. And I was okay with that!

I loved all of these people. I didn't mind what they thought of me.

I was in a good mood!

And then—

I saw infinity.

I genuinely heard a bass drop. The concrete rumbled through my boots.

Time stopped.

He gazed into my eyes. I couldn't breathe. He gazed, and everything was still. All the giant screens froze. Planet Earth actually stopped rotating. He was closer than the smaller bronze statue—but right now, everybody was a statue. It was all frozen.

His eyes were the most beautiful eyes I had ever seen.

I breathed.

All was still.

Something moved, slowly. People around us moved, slowly. The world resumed itself.

I tried breathing, though my heart pounded in my throat. I took a step forward.

He held my gaze.

I smiled—

He looked away.

My heart sank! His cheek was so beautiful. He looked at something over his shoulder. But I couldn't look away.

His hair was jet black. His skin was like the surface of the moon. He was half a foot taller than me. He was lean.

I gazed up at him, willing him to look back. I don't know whether I stood still, or moved.

He looked around himself. It was like he tried not to smile. Or did I imagine it?

I stared on. Somehow, I knew he wasn't creeped out.

Now we were close. Had I moved toward him? Or had he moved toward me?

I could have checked the bronze statues for reference. But I didn't want to. There was something inevitable about it all.

He looked at me.

Again, I saw infinity in his eyes.

Chapter 4

It was infinite eye contact. Xavier and I connected!

But I want to tell you about Sage Knox. I had a lot of friends. Yet somehow, no one knew me like Sage knew me. The opposite was true too. No one knew Sage like I knew Sage. We were close friends ever since the seventh grade. We'd gone to New York University together too. I was okay with people calling us *best friends*. We were! I had other best friends: Isabel, and Devonte. Sage had Mia. Just because someone was your best friend, it didn't mean that that person was better than all of your other friends. Basically, I considered everyone to be my friend! But at the end of the day, I only had Sage, and a few others.

We hung out as often as we could. Given our careers, it was usually something like twice a month. I knew Sage's friends and family and Sage knew mine. But we didn't belong to any group. Though Sage was close with some of my friends, and though I knew most of hers, it was essentially just *Sage and me*. Just the two of us. We liked it that way.

Anyway. The following week, I was with Sage at a party! It was her ex-boss's startup launch, coinciding with his birthday. Luis had extended invitations to his colleagues' colleagues, to his friends' friends. I was Sage's non-romantic plus-one.

We were at the Rainbow Room in Midtown. Luis had hired the immense space on the 65th floor of Rockefeller Center. Canapés were served. Soon, there would be speeches.

I liked parties. Sage, not so much. I guess she'd invited me because she hadn't wanted to go alone. I guess I was lucky.

"I said, 'No it's not.' And she said, 'Yes it is.' And I'm like—'Uh, *no it's not*.' Do you know what I mean? She wouldn't let it go."

"Don't listen to people like that."

"I know, but it's just annoying!" Sage muttered. "She's my superior, but she can't give away my job. It was my job. Not only that, I *wanted* to do that job."

"You were right," I said. "Shush, she's coming."

Sage froze.

"How are you, darling?"

Sage whirled around. She leaned back, looked at her colleague. "Not bad, not bad." Blinked her thick eyelashes.

The woman smiled. "Nice party, right?"

"It's nice." Sage looked at me. "Abigail, this is my friend Rachael."

Abigail shook my hand. She thought we would get along.

"Now, are you the one that works with Citigroup?"

I nodded.

"Look at you!" Abigail looked me up and down. "And so young…"

"We're basically the same age," Sage told her.

"So young," Abigail repeated. "You know, you'd love American Express. Actually, my director over there—" She gestured, blond hair sweeping.

"She's happy in her role," Sage interrupted.

I widened my eyes. Sage gave me a look that said, 'Trust me.'

"You're an analyst, right?" Abigail asked.

I glanced at Sage.

"What kind of analyst are you, Rachael?"

"MSS." I immediately regretted answering.

"I see. Your skills would be useful with us."

"That sounds good."

Sage facepalmed.

"But I'm asking a lot of questions." Abigail stepped back. "I'm sure my subordinate has told you all about me already?"

"Um, she might have?"

"Then you'll know I'm all sunshine." Abigail grinned, winning me over. "Sage, why don't you introduce your friend to Michael?"

"She's happy in her role," Sage hissed.

"Michael, look what I found. Now, Rachael here—"

Michael joined our circle.

"One second," Sage told Michael, holding up a finger.

She pulled me by my wrist into the hallway.

I waited.

"I've got you on this one."

"I don't see the issue," I told my best friend. "You know I hate my job."

"We all hate our jobs." Breath hot like arancini. "You're not working at American Express."

"It's not like anything's actually going to happen. I go to these parties all the time."

Sage sighed.

"Imagine if we worked together!" I chirped. "We could walk in Rockefeller Park at lunch!"

"That would be nice," Sage conceded.

"Nothing's going to happen."

"You're right. I just *really* don't want you to work with Abigail. It's worse than you think."

"I know. We're just talking. Relax."

"Hold up."

I waited.

"I just need a second."

"Of course."

Sage's heavy breathing slowed.

"Just let me know when you're ready."

Sage regained herself. She checked her deep wine lipstick in the mirror. She looked into my eyes.

"Gorgeous," I told her.

I followed Sage back into the light.

"Look, he's already forgotten about me," I said. Sage looked at Michael, shouting with several men, all laughing.

"She hasn't." Sage glanced through her lashes.

"Abigail!"

"You know, you're here with the best." Abigail smiled. Gestured. "Do you know what that is?"

"Of course."

By the window was Christophe Le Caillec, CFO of American Express.

"And what about—that?"

"Brenda Tsai. State Street."

Abigail looked at me. "Very good! You've certainly been around."

"Sure."

"Now, did you want to meet Michael?"

"I'd love to."

But now Abigail's attention was stolen by a handsome young man. They joked. So I played Abigail's game with Sage.

"Do you know who—that is?" I gestured to a well-known Berkshire Hathaway executive.

"Doesn't everyone?"

"And her?" It was a Berkshire Hathaway officer.

"Nope."

"What about—him?" I had a sixth sense for BlackRock employees.

"Don't know, don't care."

"And—this one?" Vanguard snakes lurked.

"Can we do something else?"

I knew Sage was impatient for the speeches. I wondered why she had accepted Luis's invitation. Surely she hadn't invested in his startup? There was no way she had a crush on Luis, either.

"What made you want to come to this party?"

"To be honest, I have a crush on Luis."

I laughed. "C'mon, what's the real reason?"

"Well, it's a nice change, I guess."

I nodded.

"And we don't see each other enough."

"That makes sense. You knew I'd come."

"Right. I knew you'd come. Although, I'm starting to wish I hadn't invited you."

"That hurts my feelings." It did!

"Girl, please. To be honest, I came to this party specifically with you, because I wanted to introduce you to someone." Sage looked deep into my eyes.

I looked back. Then I understood what she meant. I hadn't told Sage about Xavier yet. I hadn't told anyone.

"Really?"

Sage nodded, dark eyes large and glimmering.

"Who?"

"He..." Sage scanned the room. "...he's over by that wooden counter."

He.

"*He?* Again?"

"I mean, I've introduced you to women before."

"One, maybe."

"I've introduced you to multiple women."

"Why don't you introduce me to nonbinary folk?"

"I will." Sage sighed. "You know, you should be introducing *me* to people."

"I do!"

"You *have.*"

"I *will.*"

"C'mon, let's go." Sage took my wrist again, stepped ahead through guests. I followed.

But the crowd hushed.

Chapter 5

Sage and I looked where everyone else looked. The new company's violet logo burned into the wall. An Amex executive stood beside the projection, grinning over a microphone.

"It'll have to wait," Sage whispered.

She hadn't let go of my wrist. Who was at the cherry counter? And why did Sage want to introduce us?

"...It has been such a privilege to watch you develop into the man you are today," the executive boomed. "American Express is not the same without you. But look around the room. I believe it is clear that Ultra has the full support of American Express."

Everyone clapped.

"So, it is my complete and absolute honor, to present to you all: Luis Medina."

Luis accepted the microphone. Throughout the host's presentation, most guests gave him their undivided attention. Sage watched and listened, but kept looking over her shoulder at the cherrywood counter. I watched the presentation, barely listening.

There were three more speakers. The violet images were nice. Someone mentioned vesting schedule optionality. Finally, Luis took the microphone. Sage exhaled.

"On and up, my friends."

"On and up," guests chanted.

I tried not to roll my eyes.

"Yes. So, the party will go for a few more hours. This is still the City that never sleeps."

A rush of joy emanated throughout the room. COVID-19 hadn't hurt our City. It was 2024.

"...yourself, and coconut-ice marshmallows will be served, and cheesecakes..."

Luis's voice was drowned out by music and chatter. He danced into the crowd.

"This way." Sage squeezed my wrist.

"Why do you want me to meet this guy so bad?"

"I just do. Wait 'til you meet him."

"I'm coming, just relax!"

Sage pulled me through expensively-dressed bodies.

"Well isn't this a surprise?" Someone smiled and waved.

"Oh, hey Ronald!" Politely I smiled at the floorboards.

"Where are you going?" His scent was of moss and sclarene.

"She's coming with me!" Sage snapped over her shoulder.

I giggled.

Now Sage tried to get someone's attention. I placed my hand on the cherry counter.

"Hi, how are you?"

We locked eyes...

...the party disappeared.

The only movement was his perfect head sweeping from side to side.

He tried to get my attention. He didn't need to—he had it! His crystalline eyes explored, as though searching for signs of consciousness. I realized my mouth gaped. I shut it.

Had this moment been preordained?

He was so tall, I made out the ceiling in my periphery. I wanted to touch his perfect stubble. His smile was genuine, and deep. His eyes made me want to cry. His hair was gold, like dark sand. He'd gotten his Ivy League cut that morning. Right?

Slowly, I became aware of Sage violently shaking my left arm.

"...Good." That was all I managed.

"Harry." His hand emerged.

"Rachael." I reached upward.

His strength was implicit. Gently, he took my hand.

"Are you okay?"

The man was genuinely concerned.

I mumbled.

"Rachael." Sage laughed in my ear.

I severed eye contact with the man and saw Sage cover her mouth, high-pitched sounds escaping her fingers as she turned away.

"Are you—crying?" I asked. Giggling.

"I—"

Tears welled in her eyes as she failed to suppress her laughter.

"Do you two need a minute?" the man asked.

We did! Sage snorted. Her noises were so familiar. They triggered uncontrollable laughter! The two of us couldn't stop. I was embarrassed because the tall handsome man stood right there. Especially when tears fell from my eyes!

"I'll give you a minute," Harry said. He faced the server opposite the counter.

"Breathe," Sage tried to say. "Breathe, okay?"

I looked across, terrified the tall man might hear us.

Looking back at Sage, I tried to shush her, holding my finger to my quivering lips.

"He can't hear us," Sage whispered in my ear.

I tried indicating that he *could*.

"Babe, the way you *stared*—"

I jerked Sage away from the counter.

"He can hear you!"

"Chill!"

We wrestled with our laughter.

"What happened? Why did you black out like that?" Sage snorted.

"I didn't black out!"

"Girl, you *blacked out*!"

Sage and I snickered uncontrollably!

At last, our breathing slowed.

Sage blew through puckered lips.

"Can we try again?" she asked.

"Is he still there?"

"He hasn't moved."

I stole a glance. Sage followed my eyes. Harry sat patiently in his custom-tailored shirt. His big fingers crossed neatly on the cherrywood counter. Completely oblivious, he stared at the glowing wall.

We immediately exploded into fresh laughter.

Chapter 6

"Take two?" Sage urged over the music.

"He's too tall!"

"You're never like this," Sage frowned suspiciously. "You're *Rachael Ellery*. You're never shy!"

"He's too attractive, Sage!"

"*C'mon!*"

Random heads turned.

"Let's go, girl." Sage's breath was hot in my ear. She gripped me, left elbow. Forced me back to the polished counter.

We stood next to the man. Side-by-side like little toys. Seated, Harry was still taller than us.

"Harry, this is Rachael. Rachael, Harry."

I squeaked at Harry.

Awkward silence! All around us, businesspeople celebrated. The party was loud. Yet I definitely heard crickets chirp.

Sage cleared her throat.

"Harry works for JPMorgan Chase."

I looked at her luminous eyes.

What was she trying to tell me?

"You can say that again!" Harry cried.

I looked in Harry's sky eyes. I felt like I was flying.

"Youzempriapiboutha!" I giggled.

More silence.

More crickets.

"Sorry?" Harry looked at Sage, confused.

Sage let out a sigh. "Did you want to repeat that?"

Sage knew exactly what I'd tried to say to Harry. She was forcing me to speak for myself.

I took a deep breath.

"You seem pretty happy about that."

Sage's laughter overflowed again.

"Yes, I am," Harry replied. "I am *very* happy about that." His smile was delicious.

"About working for JPMorgan Chase?"

"*Mmhm*." Harry nodded enthusiastically. "My work constitutes my blood and my soul. We're the largest bank in the *world* by market capitalization..."

"You *were*," Sage corrected. "Last year."

"Er, thanks for that, Sage." Harry blinked. "I mean, we're *indisputably* the largest bank in the United States."

"By assets you're about the fifth-largest bank in the world," I encouraged. "Three-point-nine trillion, or something. You're consistently ranked highly by *Forbes*."

"Well, of course we are!" Harry grinned. Somehow, his speaking voice was humble!

"Don't get him started on investment banking," Sage warned.

Harry's laugh was huge, yet elegant. Like a magnificent waterfall.

"Well, enough about me," Harry said, rotating on his stool to face us. "You must be with the wonderful Amex?"

It was a light joke. JPMorgan Chase and American Express tended not to partner.

"Citibank," I answered.

"*Aha.*"

"We're TBTF."

"You certainly are."

"Isn't Citi launching in China soon?" Sage asked.

"I love China, I hope so."

"China..." Harry began, shaking his head.

"None of that's important, anyway," I dismissed. I hated my job, I hated banks. I hated all of it.

"It most definitely *is* important," Harry said, eyes twinkling like the sky. "There's no need to downplay the incredible work that you do."

"Thanks, I guess." He knew nothing about the work that I did.

"So, Rachael." He leaned forward. Gazed into my eyes. My entire body tingled. "If you don't mind me asking, what role are you in?"

Sage turned on her heel. "I'll leave you to it."

"Hang on."

Sage paused. I took her arm. She stayed.

"Risk and control," I told Harry, arm-in-arm with Sage.

Sage seemed exasperated, yet resigned. She accepted me, and the countless quirks I came with.

"Do you need moral support?" Harry smiled.

"No, but Sage is staying here."

"May I ask why?"

"Because I am," Sage answered.

Harry paused.

"Makes sense," he shrugged. He cleared his throat. "Now, risk and control. You're a smart woman, then."

Sage rolled her eyes so hard I felt it through our linked arms.

"Not really," I answered. "It's kind of a dumb job, to be honest."

"So, why do you do it?"

I looked around at the circular tables, at the sweating faces. Considered his question.

"It's a job."

"So, you like money," Harry informed me.

"No," I said. "But I like eating, I like having... somewhere to stay."

"Do you have pets?"

Sage gripped my arm.

"What?"

Sage gave me her glowing eyes again.

I whispered in her ear. "I thought you were trying to introduce him to me?"

"Don't mind me," Harry said, annoyed.

Sage whispered in my ear. "I was. But I'm starting to regret it."

"Why?"

"It's fine. Trust me! It's fine." It was strange. *Right now, Sage's eyes glowed far deeper and more beautifully than Harry's.*

"Sorry," I said to Harry. "Pets. Yeah, I have a puppy."

"Did I say the wrong thing?"

I realized Harry's question was genuine.

"No, you didn't," I assured him.

He relaxed a little.

"I have a puppy."

"You said that."

"I said it twice."

"You must have a puppy, then."

I looked at Sage, laughing. I realized she wasn't even paying attention. It was like she always said: the world didn't revolve around me.

"How'd you know?" I asked Harry.

"I believe that you told me," Harry said. A gold eyebrow raised. He was slowly catching on to my sense of humor.

"Told you what?"

"That you had a puppy," Harry smiled.

"Yes!"

I started clapping.

"You didn't tell me his name."

"That wasn't an accident."

"Please tell me his name."

If Harry's aroma hadn't been so tantalizing, I might have left. He was a lot.

"What if I... told you the first letter?"

"Can I go now?" Sage asked, politely.

Harry laughed, like a waterfall splashing.

"Only if you *need* to," I said.

"I'll be back."

I let go of Sage's body. She vanished into the crowd. My arm felt cold where Sage had been.

"So," Harry said. "What's the first letter of your little boy's name, then?"

"Okay." I folded my arms. "First of all, they use they/them pronouns. Second of all—"

"They/them pronouns!" Harry scoffed.

Disappointment pushed at my heart!

"You're talking about Sage?"

"I mean my puppy."

Harry burst out laughing.

Then he saw I was serious.

"Okay." Harry's gold eyebrows folded in. "Your puppy uses—" I watched Harry try with all of his might to be serious. "Fine. So, what's the first letter of his name?"

"Their name."

"Sorry, what's the first letter of—their name?"

I smiled.

"It's 'V.'"

"'V.'" Harry pondered. "Is your puppy's name... Vincent?"

"No."

I smiled, placing my arm on the gleaming counter. I looked up at him.

Harry stroked his chin. I liked his attentiveness. Despite everything, Harry was downright charming.

"Is it... Vance?"

I cringed.

"No. Um, why are you guessing my puppy's name, dude?"

"Is there something else you want to talk about?"

We had no obligation to talk, whatsoever. But I didn't mind.

"This is fine, I suppose."

Our eyes connected.

I melted.

"One more guess."

Several seconds stretched.

"Vaughn?"

I retched.

"Three strikes and you're out."

"Okay. You have to tell me now."

I inhaled.

"It's Victory."

Harry immediately burst into laughter. "No." Harry's chuckling slowed. "No, that's a wonderful name."

"They're a wonderful puppy."

"I'm sure he is."

"They."

"My deepest apologies. I'm sure they're a wonderful puppy."

"Victory is the best puppy in the world!"

"I believe you."

"Maybe... you won't have to."

I froze. I couldn't believe I'd just said it.

"How do you mean?"

"I meant nothing. Sorry."

He gazed down into my eyes. His sandpaper stubble was so near. There was no denying it: we felt good.

Eye contact.

Harry inhaled.

"Well, if you meant nothing..."

Harry exhaled. His breath felt like I swam in cool water.

"...then you meant nothing."

Yet for the first time that night, I felt like I meant something.

Chapter 7

Snow continued falling. Grey sludge covered the streets. The City remained freezing.

I met Xavier Pang at Ariston Coffee Bar in Greenwich Village. It was a fabulous flower shop serving ethically-sourced Colombian coffee. It was the fourth time we met.

As usual, I arrived early. As usual, he arrived late.

But for the first time, I controlled my breathing when I saw him. It still shortened, there was still that vertiginous feeling. Yet this time, I controlled it all.

Xavier was large. He was muscular. Yet Xavier was slender. He walked with the elegance of a dancer. Today he wore a denim overcoat with a plush hood. I didn't want to know if that fur was real. He hadn't noticed me yet. I watched him eye the dazzling flower arrangements.

Our eyes connected and we smiled. Gracefully, he stepped to my table.

"Nice place, right?"

"It's beautiful."

He removed the overcoat and slipped it on the coat rack. He carefully took his seat.

"How was your day?"

"Okay, so far. I'm gonna get the cortado."

"Oh, I might get one of those."

"But what about your—?"

"I'm in the mood."

I watched. "Are you sure?"

Xavier nodded.

I watched. "Okay."

I always wondered whether Xavier was uncomfortable with my staring, which I couldn't help. But he was used to it. He'd told me so. And I could tell he really *was* comfortable with being stared at.

Xavier stayed at our table, and I ordered at the counter.

"I'll do two cortados."

But Xavier was behind me.

"Actually, I'll get an espresso shot."

I rolled my eyes.

"So, one cortado, one espresso shot?" the red-haired server asked.

I looked at Xavier.

"Yes," he smiled.

I paid. It was my turn.

"*Xiaoxianrou*," Xavier said, back at our table.

I tried to pronounce it.

"*Xiao*," Xavier said.

"*Xiao*," I copied.

"*Xian*."

"*Xian*."

"*Rou*."

"*Rou!*"

"Yes."

"So, they're calling you this," I said. "But you—*don't* like the label?"

"It is what it is."

"So, you're okay with being called that?"

Xavier shrugged.

He was being cryptic. It wasn't the Chinese word. It was his refusal to answer my question. Xavier was cryptic. I was beginning to accept it.

"What does it mean?"

Xavier laughed.

"Little fresh meat."

I stared.

"Are you kidding me?"

"No."

Xavier was a model. He'd done it for more than ten years. We were the same age. At some point, I worked out that he'd started modeling during high school.

And he was paid.

Well.

Surrounded by flowers, our conversation took on a life of its own. It was so natural. I was never unsure what to say.

"I still can't believe we met in Times Square."

"One day, you will believe it."

"Of all places. Times Square! My absolute favorite place. The *one* place you would be *least* likely to meet someone."

"The place everyone hates."

"The place everyone loves! The place every New Yorker hates."

"The place everyone hates except you and me."

"Except you and me!"

Xavier laughed. "I was just on my way home from the theater."

"*Aladdin.*"

"The musical. And I was just standing there."

"Looking fine as hell."

"And then I saw you."

"I saw you."

"You did."

"You saw me too."

"How could I not have noticed? You were staring at me!"

"Everyone stares at you."

"But you were looking at me differently."

"Did I creep you out?"

"No."

We were laughing.

"Seriously, though. *Aladdin*?"

"My friend was in it."

"I know. But Xavier—*Aladdin*?"

"It's not bad. You should go see it."

"You wanna go together?"

"I've seen it."

Laughing, laughing.

"Do you stand around in Times Square very often?"

"Only on my way home from the theater."

"How often is that?"

"Every now and then."

"But didn't it feel like it was supposed to happen?"

"What?"

"Like, how we met in Times Square. Didn't it sort of feel like it was—planned?"

"I get what you mean. Yes."

"*There*, you said, 'Yes.'"

"You forced me to."

"But you said it."

"I did."

"I feel like you meant it."

Xavier was silent.

I waited for him to speak, but he didn't.

"So did you mean it?"

Xavier looked at me.

"Yes."

"Every time you look in my eyes—"

"Actually, I don't like eye contact."

Always laughing.

"No one likes eye contact."

"Except you."

"No," I said. "I don't like eye contact."

"You *love* eye contact."

"Yeah. But—not always."

Xavier waited for me to speak.

"Sometimes it's weird."

"Depends who it's coming from."

"And the situation, and the context. You know. But for the most part, I like eye contact."

"You *love* eye contact."

"I do."

Chatter around us. Lots of couples. Soothing music.

Xavier spoke, his lips beautiful. "You know, we're probably the only two New Yorkers who like Times Square."

"You've said that before."

"I'm saying it again."

"It's true."

His thin facial muscles moved.

"What do you like about it?"

He thought for a while. "It makes me feel..."

"Alive."

"Not exactly."

"Sorry, I interrupted you."

"No, it's okay. Times Square is like…"

"Sorry."

"…the place with so much history. There's so much that has happened there."

"Oh, you mean the hustlers and the criminals and the—"

"Yes, but also—The New York Times. But then there was the Great Depression."

"The Depression wasn't kind to Times Square." It was my turn. "But that was later, right? It was a sweetgum forest. There was a beaver pond there. The Lenape are the rightful owners. Always will be. Then the Europeans came. I guess there was a rich man who bought the land. Then it was Longacre Square, and there were a ton of horses. Then came the train system! And at the same time, the theaters! You know they called Broadway the Great White Way?"

"You're kidding."

"Because of the lights."

"Oh."

"Yeah, because of all the lights. Allegedly. But it was becoming the Theater District. *Then* they built the Times Tower. That's where the New York Times was, and now it's where they do the ball drop on New Year's Eve."

"I thought that was One Times Square?"

"Let me speak. It's the same thing. Like, they're two different names for the same building. But the Times moved down the block. As in, the newspaper. *Then* there was the Great Depression. And the theaters went out of business and the other types of theaters moved in. The ones I don't like talking about. There were all sorts of people there. They did—well, you know what they did. Burlesque, and—yeah. Then there was World War Two." I sighed. "Then there was the Counterculture in the 60s. But the good hippies didn't go to Times Square. The bad ones went there. Not that I think anyone's really bad. But—Times Square had a bad reputation. It was crime central. They played three-card monte, essentially a con game. You just didn't go to Times Square. Then there was the epidemic."

"Like—the acronym?"

"No. Well, yeah. But I meant the other one. The epidemic."

"Oh."

"I don't like talking about it. But you know what I'm saying. But then there was the 90s, and we were born."

"Yeah. You know, it wasn't that bad in the 70s and 80s."

"Maybe not for you."

"I wasn't there. But it wasn't as dangerous as you think."

"Again—maybe not for you."

"What's that supposed to mean?"

"Well, you're a man."

"You'll learn more about me."

"I'm looking forward to it. But in the 90s, *we* were born. Yay! And Times Square became nice! It wasn't all because of Giuliani. My dad says it was a citywide effort. They made it a place for children, and families, and people visiting New York, and..."

"You and me."

"Well, yeah. And it's *nice* now."

"Keep your voice down."

"You don't have to be ashamed about liking Times Square."

"Fine, I like Times Square."

"Right? I like it too."

"We're probably the only two New Yorkers who like Times Square."

"Yeah. How many times are you going to say that?"

"I'll probably say it a few more times."

Somehow, our conversation had lightened up again.

Chapter 8

There was something about him.

I couldn't explain it. Someone could talk to Xavier and think he lacked personality. Honestly, he didn't say much. But there was just *something about him*. It wasn't his physical beauty. Well—there was *that*. But there was *something else*. Xavier was special. At work, I often felt trapped—but then I'd remember Xavier. And I just couldn't stop thinking about him.

I needed to figure him out.

That Tuesday, we did something very romantic. We protested in support of Julian Assange. I'm not sure how it happened. I was working from home, and wanted a walking buddy. So I asked Xavier. He'd just finished his daily workout, and agreed. We ended up on Second Avenue, and saw the large group. Handmade signs. A mobile billboard. Chanting.

We joined in.

"Free Julian Assange! Free Julian Assange! Free Julian Assange!"

It was me more than Xavier. I think he felt uncomfortable. But he told me he didn't.

I knew the story. Assange was probably a hero. There were the Swedish charges, but I gave Assange the benefit of the doubt. Chelsea Manning was probably a hero too. And I learned more from the speeches at the rally. In 2024, no one talked about Julian Assange anymore. Meanwhile, Assange spent every minute of his life in His Majesty's Prison Belmarsh. His living conditions were terrible. If extradited to the United States, he likely faced the death penalty. I didn't like thinking about these things. So I protested.

"Free Julian Assange! Free Julian Assange! Free Julian Assange!"

"C'mon, let's go," Xavier said.

We went around the corner. We found a long concrete strip under a canopy of branches. The place was gorgeous.

"How come you wanted to leave?"

"Do you know what Julian Assange did in Sweden?"

"I'm familiar with the accusations. Let's not talk about it."

"Fine."

We walked deeper into the little walkway.

"Can we sit here?"

"Sure."

We sat on a park bench. A sign read: "KATHARINE HEPBURN GARDEN."

"Do you think protesting actually works?" I asked.

"I thought we weren't going to talk about it."

"I mean, in general. Like, demonstrating. Marching. Do you think it actually works?"

Xavier sat to my left. He wore a black hoodie, comfortable-looking blue jeans, and black Adidas sneakers. A stud bedazzled his right earlobe. I knew it was all expensive, and this was only his everyday wear. I wondered if he felt cold. When he thought, his narrowed eyes made me shiver. I couldn't look away from his profile, backgrounded by pavers and pin oaks. His lips were full. Everything else about his features was so slender. Delicate. I wanted to look at Xavier's eyes... eternally.

"I don't know if it works," Xavier said, finally.

"Do you go to protests?"

"Never."

"Why not?"

"I don't know if they work."

"I go to protests sometimes," I said. "I feel strongly about certain things. And if I can add my voice, I will."

"But these problems are so big. These are huge issues. What can we do?"

"The world is huge. You know what? The universe is huge."

Xavier's laugh was better than music.

"I went to a protest the other week," I said. "For Palestine. What the U.S. is doing is not right."

"No. It's not right. But there is a protest every single week. And we are still backing Israel."

"And Biden is literally *eating*—"

"He will continue to eat—"

"You're saying I shouldn't protest, right?"

"Why?"

"Well, why do anything?" I threw my hands up. "If I can add my voice, I will. That's what I'm saying. Why do anything? Do you have any clue how big the universe is?"

"Actually, I have no idea."

"You know it's big."

"Of course."

"It's bigger than you can possibly imagine, Xavier! You know what, you're right. What's happening in Gaza, what's happening in Ukraine, what's happening in Myanmar and Senegal and Yemen is out of our control. You know what? *Everything* is out of our control. People think they have agency, right? I'm not talking about your modeling agencies. I'm talking about free will. You know what I mean. We get put here on Earth, and we think we can choose things. We think our choices are ours. But it's sort of like a beautiful illusion. We can't actually do anything."

"I know what you mean."

"You *do*, and that's why I like you."

"So, that's why you protest."

"That's beside the point. But actually, we *can* choose things."

"Of course we can."

"No, but we *can't*."

"People go marching, and screaming, and the wars go on."

"But even the wars are insignificant!" I couldn't believe I'd just said it. "Do you know how many people are alive? There are more than eight billion of us now. *Eight billion.* That means that more than 99% of people are *not* affected by wars. Less than 80 million of us are directly affected. Sure, there are 146 million people in Russia right? But most are doing okay. I *know* it. This is what no one is saying. Why do people focus on the bad things? How about we focus on the good things? The planet is just going to keep on spinning. It doesn't care. And this is actually a *beautiful* thing. Do you know how *beautiful* the universe is? It's just nice blackness and some stars and planets and some nice things. And on one of the planets, there are people. Eight billion of us. And less than 1% of us are attacking one another and more than 99% of us are just peacefully living our lives. Do you know what I mean? I think it's nice. We're born, and then we get to learn to walk and talk. We make friends. We get to eat food! We fall in love. We make families. Some of us get to grow old, and watch our children have children! We get to feel warm sunlight and walk in soft grass. There are little green trees and a whole lot of blue water. I know it's not blue, dude. But do you know how lucky we are to have trees and water? Trees and water don't exist *anywhere* else in the entire universe. And people want to complain because less than 1% of other people—people they don't even know—are fighting. *Of course* we should fix the problems. There are so many problems. I don't even want to go into them. The world has problems. So we should do what we can. We should add our voices. But you're literally *one in eight billion*, Xavier. You're totally right. Protesting achieves nothing. I'm just one in eight billion, too. But I can add my voice. Why not do it? Why not protest? You can't actually choose anything. If you eat salad instead of a bagel for lunch tomorrow, you're still a tiny person on a giant planet. And that's a tiny planet in a giant Milky Way galaxy. And that's a tiny galaxy in an incomprehensibly giant universe! What the hell is a street rally? You could eat salad for lunch tomorrow, and the world would just keep on spinning. You could discover the secret to world peace tomorrow, and the world would just keep on spinning! It doesn't care. And that's kind of *beautiful*, don't you think? I think it is, anyway. Because free will simultaneously *exists* and *doesn't exist*. It's not just a beautiful illusion. Guess what? If you decide to eat salad tomorrow, you *will* eat salad tomorrow! It's like magic. It's not gonna affect any stars.

But you're still *choosing*. We can talk about free will forever and ever so I might stop. It's circular, right? But I just think it's nice to know that whatever you choose to do, the stars are gonna be okay. There are so many terrible things happening in the world right now—but the Andromeda Galaxy doesn't mind. It's gonna be okay. You might say, 'Oh, well, there are no people in the Andromeda Galaxy. There's no life there.' And to that I would answer, 'Most people here on Earth are gonna be okay, too.' You need to trust the Human Development Index. The *vast* majority of people have enough food for the rest of the week. They have places to stay, they live in safe conditions with their families. They don't live like we live. But they're safe. Numbers don't lie. It's not even optimism. It's statistics. We do good research. Rigorous research. And by 'We,' I mean humanity. I like reading the official data. We need to focus on the good things."

"I sort of get what you mean. People like to complain. It's kind of nice to think about how big the universe is. Who knows, maybe it's beautiful?"

"It's beautiful! I can't believe you're even listening to me. Do you think I'm crazy?"

"No, I don't think you're crazy."

"I don't know why you make me feel like opening up. But the universe is so glorious and magnificent and all the stars are glimmering. And people want to complain—but not all the time! Sometimes people are hopeful!"

"I try to be hopeful."

"And I think it's kind of *nice* to know how small we are. We're so cute! And all the stars are dancing, and all the asteroids are laughing, and us humans are so little and smol and cute. Haha!"

"But it's sort of sad, too," Xavier said. "To think about how smol we are. We're almost powerless. That's what you're saying, right? For instance, I can choose to—I don't know—eat something different. But it doesn't change anything."

"The stars don't mind what you eat."

"Right. But that's kind of—sad."

"Yeah."

"The problems in the world are so big. What can I do?"

"You can try."

"Right. But what's the point in trying? It's like you said. The world is—enormous."

"The universe."

"Right. The universe. It's enormous."

Xavier sighed.

Now I felt sad.

Xavier did too, I think.

We were silent for a while.

The traffic was noisy and pointless.

The wind was so cold.

"I'm insignificant," I said, finally.

My words faded into the winter air.

I felt a weight in my chest.

The trees around us were leafless.

"There's one thing you said." Xavier looked at me.

I was already looking back.

"'I'm just one in eight billion.' You said that. Well actually, Rachael, you and I are *two* in eight billion."

My heart.

"Two in eight billion."

Tears filled my eyes.

I looked away.

"Look at me." His voice was so gentle.

For some reason, I shook my head.

But then I felt his hand on my thigh. It was the subtlest feeling. I felt his heat, even through several layers of clothing.

I didn't feel sad anymore.

I looked at Xavier's beautiful eyes.

"Do you have any idea how amazing you are?" Xavier's voice was low.

He had never spoken to me in this way. I gazed through my waterworks.

Eye contact through tears of joy.

"Are you crying?" I asked.

"No."

"Then what's that?" I brushed my fingertip across Xavier's black lashes.

He barely flinched. But now my fingertip was damp.

"I don't know." His lips turned up.

"Xavier, you're crying."

"Rachael, *you* are crying."

"*Why* though?"

"I don't know."

Then we were laughing, and laughing!

We cried tears of laughter, and I did not understand why.

"I have a theory," I said, at last.

"Oh no, another one?"

I pushed his shoulder, hard.

"Let me hear it."

"I believe that eye contact is the antidote to the insignificance of being human."

"Woah."

"No, really. The world is enormous. And since you're one in eight billion, you're basically insignificant. But when you look in someone else's eyes... it's like you said. Suddenly you're *two* in eight billion."

"'Someone else?'"

"Yeah, as in, any other human. When you make eye contact, you feel significant. It's self-realization. You exist in the eyes of the other."

"'The other?'"

"The other person!"

"What about me?"

Suddenly I felt really guilty.

"Yes, you, Xavier, that's what I mean. You. *You* make me feel significant."

"I'm glad I can be of service."

I pushed at his shoulder again.

"You make me feel amazing," I said. "But *eye contact*. Eye contact is the great universal language! And it's basically like, time stops. Eye contact transcends time. It *exists beyond* time! It's eternity. Eye contact for any amount of time is eternal. It's infinite. And it's the solution to the problem of only being one in eight billion."

"Eye contact."

"It's the answer!"

"It's the solution to the world's problems."

"Well—it's the solution to the problem of the insignificance that comes with being a miniscule human being in an impossibly gigantic universe. And—when you make eye contact, everything happens all at once! You're not just looking at that person's eyes. You're looking at every minute—every second—of that person's life. *A whole other person!* You connect, infinitely. Eye contact is infinite. It goes forever. Longer than forever. Eye contact is eternal."

"Being with you is eternal."

"Well thanks, Xavier."

He looked at me.

"Do you think I'm beautiful?" I asked.

"Yes. You are beautiful."

"Tell me why?"

"Your face is beautiful. Your mouth. And your blue eyes, Rachael. Your hair. Your body. You are perfect."

"Thanks."

I sighed.

"But actually, I've got a problem."

"No you don't."

"I do. Actually, I—"

I stopped.

Was now the time to tell him?

"What is it?"

"I—"

"You don't have to tell me if you don't want."

But now, I knew that I wanted to tell him.

"I love everything."

"And that's a problem?"

"I mean, like, I love *everything*. It makes it hard."

"It makes what hard?"

"Life. And—loving someone. Because—I love everyone."

Xavier laughed.

"No," I said. "I mean it. I intentionally love everyone. And I intentionally love everything. Do you think I'm crazy?"

Xavier's eyes narrowed. "No, I don't think you're crazy. But I don't think that you love everything."

"No, I promise you, I do."

"Okay. You love everything, then."

"Yeah. But do you *believe* me?"

"Yes."

I sighed. Now, he knew.

Xavier's hand hadn't left my thigh. I rested my head on his shoulder. We'd never been so intimate. I even closed my eyes. He smelled like the universe. I felt perfectly relaxed. And now, I felt warm.

"Are you okay?" I had to make sure.

"Yes." His voice vibrated in his strong chest, in my ear.

I looked up at him, and our eyes met again.

Pure infinity.

Chapter 9

But then there was Harry.

I wasn't looking for anything. That was the thing. I'd been single for two years. My last relationship hadn't been great. And to be honest, I was enjoying being single! I was 27. I had time. At some point after my last breakup, I'd gotten used to being single. I liked the feeling. It made me feel like me.

But then I met Xavier.

And a week later, I met Harry.

I liked both.

I talked it through with Isabel. I talked it through with Devonte. I talked it through with a bunch of people.

But I really didn't want to talk about it with Sage. I knew that if Sage and I talked about someone, there was no turning back. Bringing someone up with Sage meant that person was serious. So far, nothing was serious. Not with Xavier. Not with Harry. I wanted it that way. My heart really wanted me to tell Sage about Xavier! But I wouldn't. Most of my close friends had heard me say his name. But I'd asked them not to tell Sage about him. Even if I hadn't asked, they might not have told her—Sage wasn't close with many of my friends. Anyway, I really wanted to tell her about Xavier. I knew she would love him. But I forbade myself from telling her. I wasn't ready.

The snow melted, and one Sunday, Sage and I went to The Shops at Columbus Circle. I loved that place.

My stomach growled. "What are we getting for lunch?"

Sage wore her favorite khaki New Era cap. "Momofuku!"

We took the escalator.

"Thoughts on Hugo Boss?"

I giggled, looking at Hugo Boss's multistory window display. "Um, they're okay I guess." Our escalator was positioned so that we were forced to look at the new outfits. "That's a cute blouse."

"You know the story of Hugo Boss?"

"Yeah."

"It's not pretty."

"Nope."

"You want to go after Momofuku?"

"Yep."

We found a booth in the ramen restaurant. Sage ordered kimchi, chicken ramen with pork belly, and San Pellegrino Aranciata. I ordered chicken wings, mushroom ramen, and San Pellegrino Aranciata.

"I've gotta go to Lilac." Sage spoke in between mouthfuls of ramen.

"What's that?"

"Nail salon."

"I don't think there's a nail salon in the mall?"

"It's across the road." Noodles dangled from Sage's poised chopsticks. "There's a day spa next door."

"Oh." I forked my ramen. "Let's go!"

"Later. I gotta buy some shoes."

"I wanna check out that chocolate place."

"Yeah. And I wanna see if they've got that moisturizer at Aveda."

We paid for our meals. We almost always tipped 20%.

We entered Hugo Boss on the ground floor. It wasn't crowded.

"Look at this bag!" Sage cried.

"Yes! That's cool."

"Think I should get it?"

"You shouldn't get anything."

"I've got to get something. Well, I guess I don't *got* to."

"Don't give in."

"That's the point, though."

"Yeah. But Hugo Boss sucks."

"Shush!"

"Sorry."

"They can't hear us anyway. Hugo Boss *totally* sucks. These are all white people clothes."

"Oh, is that all you've got?"

"You don't wanna start me. We're in the establishment and we're gonna be respectful." Sage heaved a sigh. "I mean, welcome to my life."

"Look at these scarves!"

"They're stunning. Wow. This one suits you."

"You think so?"

"I know so." Sage unfolded the wool and draped it over my shoulders. She looked me up and down and smacked her lips.

"I can't."

"You can buy whatever you want."

"I mean, I can *afford* it."

"Yeah, but you're not buying a Hugo Boss scarf."

We burst into giggles.

I placed the scarf back on the display.

"Look, she's gorgeous." I pointed at an AI-enhanced Black model pouting in an elegant cream jacket.

"I mean, it's working." Sage stared at the blinding advertisement. "It's working. See, if they had more models like her, they'd get a head-start on next quarter. Listen to me. High-end fashion would see significant improvement. People would actually come out of their homes. We'd get this inflation under control. Listen, babe. I'd buy it! It's working on me. Only problem is—it's Hugo Boss."

I burst into laughter.

"All they need is a few more Black models." Sage started walking.

I followed. "They need more Asian models."

"Shush, babe. We're in the establishment."

"Maybe I should say it louder."

"It doesn't work coming from you."

"Why not? If more white people demand diversity, it might actually happen."

"I guess you're right."

We exited Hugo Boss. We passed an ad for Venus et Fleur, an ad for Harry Potter, an ad for Masa.

"How's it going at Amex?" I followed Sage.

"I don't wanna talk about it." Sage walked slightly ahead.

"But I care about how you're doing."

"You're trying to take care of me?"

"I mean—yes."

Sage looked at me. "I don't know what I'm doing with my life."

"Really?"

"Why am I working at Amex?"

"You told me it was your dream job."

"It still is, I guess." Sage slowed down. I ambled beside her. "But I never thought it would be so..."

"White?"

"I knew it would be white. But I never thought... it would be like this."

"You don't have to tell me. But I'm asking."

"It's like..." Sage stopped in the middle of the mall. I stopped beside her. "There are three Black people on my team. I don't know if there are any other Black-Chinese people at the company. Like, they don't provide resources for us to connect. There's someone I've seen. Actually, there might be two. But I have no way of talking to them." Sage tried to smile. She continued walking.

"You just need to talk to them. You're amazing with people. You have nothing to be shy about."

"I know, but I hate doing that."

"Talking?"

"Like, randomly. Talking randomly to random people."

"They're your coworkers."

"They're not. They work for American Express. Other than that, we have nothing to do with each other."

"You might have a lot to do with each other!"

"I guess I should talk to them. But there would be no way to approach them. It's not the thing."

"It's not the thing at Citi either. But everyone knows me there. I just talk to everyone."

"Yeah, but you're weird. Most people don't do that. Besides—I have friends at work. It's just—they have no clue."

"How do you mean?"

"I mean they're white." Suddenly Sage was angry. "You can't understand because you're white. But I can try to explain it to you."

"You don't have to."

"Long story short. The City is white. The world is white."

"The world is not white."

"Don't interrupt me. Downtown, okay, our line of work. It's white. I might be the only person at American Express who's Black and Chinese. The only one. You have no clue what that's like. I don't expect you to. But most people aren't like you. They don't empathize. They're part of an institution. In all senses of the word. I need to maintain respectability. I need to code-switch. I need to pretend I'm someone else. I'm talking 24 hours a day, seven days a week. I'm doing it right now."

"You don't have to do it with me."

"I know. But I *choose* to. I always code-switch with you. I'm gonna stop talking. We're having a good time in the mall. Anyway, don't ask me about work." Sage laughed. "Where's Aveda?"

"Third floor."

"How do you know this mall so well?"

"I love this place."

Briefly, we walked in silence.

"This place is just ads, though," Sage said. "Ads, ads, ads. Buy me. Buy me. Buy me. What is this world we live in? What are we even doing? We all know consumerism is poison. We all know money doesn't buy happiness. So what's with these rappers?" Sage opened her palm at a billboard. "Floga. Sunglass Hut. Monica Rich Kosann. Where does it end? Even the TikTok. The Instagram. It's too much. And we *contribute*. You and me, and what we do every day. Our livelihoods. I mean, we *are* capitalism. I guess it's okay, though. Why do you love this place?"

"I love everything."

"Not this again."

"I do."

Our silence was comfortable.

"You know I love everything, right?"

"Yes, I know. I'll never understand it."

"You understand love, though."

"Sure."

"You love it when I dance?" I moved my arms.

Sage shook her head.

I danced some more!

"You're so weird."

"That hurts my feelings."

"You know that I love you, right?"

"Of course. I love you, too, Sage."

Chapter 10

There was Harry, there was Harry. Wow, there was Harry.

Who was more beautiful? Well, I guess it didn't really matter. There was no question. Xavier was more physically beautiful.

But who was more *beautiful*?

I asked myself these questions. Both were so intelligent. Both were so interesting. Both were so perfect. Xavier was *more* perfect.

But—

Harry.

I felt like I understood Harry better. I knew Harry. I had Harry. Harry had me. We were the same, in so many ways. But unlike me, he wasn't even a New Yorker. He'd grown up in Connecticut, the son of a stock exchange President. His father had served on the board of directors of the Federal Reserve Bank of New York. Harry was a winner from the starting gate. He'd never have to worry about anything. I wasn't like *that*. For every dollar I had, Harry had ten! But my family had never worried about money. Harry loved his job. I hated mine. We were so different. But we were so similar. Xavier was completely different. Xavier was at the tips of my fingers. Dodging me. Xavier was *over there*.

Harry Davis was right here.

He took me to dinner in Lenox Hill. I loved exploring our City, so I'd suggested Brooklyn. Park Slope. Bed-Stuy. Williamsburg, if that was what he wanted. I'd even suggested Staten Island! But he was fixed on the Upper East Side. It wasn't hard to understand why. Like I said: I knew Harry.

The restaurant was Italian. He wore a navy shirt with a light custom-fitted Ralph Lauren dinner jacket. He had a fresh Ivy League cut. The piercing sky eyes I knew so well. The gold stubble he'd let me touch. That Clive Christian fragrance. His deep smile.

I almost loved him.

"You look beautiful tonight."

"Thanks. You too."

"I love what you've done with your hair. Did it take a long time?"

"Really? No, I haven't really done anything."

"Are you shy?"

"No."

"Then why—"

I shrugged. "Thanks for dinner."

"We just got here. You can thank me later."

I fought not to roll my eyes. "I know that."

"I mean—" Harry hesitated. "Thank you."

"Thank me?"

"Thank you for thanking me."

We laughed.

"You definitely did something with your hair."

"Okay, I did."

"You got a blowout."

How did he know that?

"You're smiling. Just. But I had a good week. The year is looking good. I was down in Wall Street on Thursday, I saw it. Not to suggest I know better than The Street itself—but certainly, the year is looking good. And I'm getting used to that feeling. You know, the one I told you about. *Swimming*. Most people just tread water. But I *swim*. Haha. But I had a good week. I'm *swimming*—Oh, that must be my mother." His lips tightened. "I'll put my phone away."

"Do you wanna get that?"

"No, I just put my phone on silent. I'm here with you. Mom's trying to—"

"Your brother."

"Yeah, he's up from Connecticut. She—"

"I know."

"Anyway, I'm here." Eye contact. "With you."

"You are."

Harry was so, so gorgeous.

He talked about his prospects for 2024. About JPMorgan Chase. About how hard he worked. His eyes twinkled as he spoke. They darted around the lavish restaurant. Every now and then, he'd take a breath. Then he'd look in my eyes. One of us might giggle. Or just breathe. And then he'd continue talking. And his eyes would continue darting.

After we ordered, he asked me about work. I told him my job wasn't as interesting as his. He nodded. Accepted my answer. Then he told me about his mom. Whom he referred to always as his 'Mother.' He loved her, I could tell. But he would never admit it. Instead, I learned about how Harry's mom liked white wine and fig and raisins. How they called every Sunday evening. How she asserted herself in all three of her children's lives, regardless of how professional and grown-up they became. How she forced Harry to look after his younger brother while he was up from Connecticut. Regardless of how professional and grown-up Harry became.

The Davis family was powerful. Since childhood, Harry had taken his status for granted. I would never tell him. Anyway, I didn't mind. He loved money. The whole family did. Money was the fuel in the family's engine.

Yet Harry had humility. Blind to those who were less fortunate, he nevertheless evaded arrogance. He *fit in*. Maybe it was because we'd chosen the window table in one of the best restaurants in Lenox Hill. Or maybe it was just because Harry was respectful. He knew how to read the room. Again—affluent Manhattanites occupied *this particular* room. Yet somehow, I knew in my heart that Harry was for real.

Maybe this was why I loved him.

Or maybe it was his strong fingers? We tasted our meals. Yet all I thought of was those fingers. I watched them dance with his shimmering cutlery. I watched them dip his silverware-pierced Tagliolini Neri into his mouth. I watched his jaw work, his sky eyes low. He'd paused mid-sentence to chew, making me hold my breath.

His Adam's apple lifted.

Swallowing.

He continued speaking.

I exhaled.

We ordered different desserts. So, we swapped them around. Harry's Torta di Caprese was warm and delicious. We savored every bite of one another's treats. Because we didn't want the moment to end.

Some time ago, Harry's eyes had stopped darting. Now he looked only at mine. We sipped from spotless glasses. Everything felt good. Unbelievably good. My life was going so well. I couldn't believe I was here. With Harry Davis! Smiling. My chest felt warm. The night felt right. Everything felt happy!

So, when he asked if I wanted to check out his place, I agreed.

Chapter 11

It was fate. For some reason, I'd decided to leave my little Nissan at home. I'd caught the subway to the Italian restaurant. So, after Harry paid for dinner, he offered to drive me to his place.

He guided me down the pavement. I gasped when I saw the Fuji White two-door Jaguar.

Harry laughed. He opened its door.

Surely I wasn't supposed to sit inside?

"Are you serious?"

"It's an F-Type. Brand new."

Gingerly, I clambered into the passenger seat. Gently, Harry closed the door after me. He walked around to the driver's seat.

The Jaguar smelled like $100,000 American. When Harry closed his door, his Clive Christian cologne mixed in with the aroma. He drove me through Central Park, exquisite at night. We wound under tunnels covered in masses of dark green foliage.

Harry lived in a white townhouse in the Upper West Side. The entire property. I shouldn't have been surprised, yet somehow, I was.

The façade was white limestone. Harry mentioned the Flemish Renaissance. A French gargoyle watched from the fourth floor.

We walked up the white steps. He opened the glass-and-mahogany door. I stepped inside.

The door clicked, and the light came on.

I gasped.

Harry's home was *unbelievable*.

"Is everything okay?"

I struggled to answer him. This was the most impressive parlor level I'd ever seen! Did I belong here?

"Yes."

I manifested 'Yes.' I was happy. It would take time for me to settle in. But I felt happy here!

With Harry Davis.

"It's my place," Harry reminded me. "All four floors."

"No."

"Yes." He was relaxed. "Welcome."

I noticed my paralysis.

"Would you like to come upstairs?"

I shut my gaping mouth.

"Sure."

"Would you like to take the Elevette? Or the stairs?"

I swallowed.

"You choose."

"Why are you whispering?"

I shrugged.

"How about the Elevette?"

I looked at him. He smiled calmly.

I nodded.

Harry's musculature bulged in his Ralph Lauren jacket. We took his smooth home elevator to his fourth floor. The word 'penthouse' popped in my mind.

I felt dizzy.

The Elevette pinged. The doors slid open. Harry let me walk first.

I couldn't even!

"Welcome, Rachael."

His cathedral ceiling soared at least 20 feet overhead. Four massive windows looked out onto his English Garden and the brownstones across the road. Colorful cubist paintings adorned the walls. The room smelled of Harry Davis and romance. Of deep brightness.

"I love it."

I did.

"You can sit wherever you like."

I perched myself on the corner of his sofa.

I heard jazz music. I looked. He owned a glowing gramophone.

"Would you like apple slices? Pear? Or some homemade fruitcakes?"

"Sure."

"How about these wafers and this fresh gorgonzola?"

"I—"

"What would you like to drink?"

"Oh. Water?"

"Water. Still? Or seltzer?"

"Still."

"Iced? Or refrigerated. Or room temperature?

"Anything."

He placed it all on his granite-and-marble coffee table. He dimmed his brilliant lights. He sat on his sofa.

Harry's wealth overwhelmed me. More than making me like him, it impressed me. I didn't know if I belonged here.

We were silent. The rich gramophone tinkled.

I couldn't think of anything else to say:

"How old are you?"

Harry looked serious. I wanted to know why.

"Old."

I giggled.

"Yeah, I'm old."

"How old?"

"You're very blunt, aren't you?"

"I'm sorry."

"No, I'm joking."

"You don't look like you're joking."

He looked in my eyes. "Don't I?"

"You seem a bit... serious."

His crystalline eyes looked down. "Yeah."

I tried not to giggle. "I mean, you don't have to answer."

"I'm 38."

I hid my shock. "You're not old."

His eyes glinted. "I'm not young."

"You're not as young as me."

"That's what I mean." Suddenly I noticed his crow's feet.

"Well, that explains this place."

Harry shook his head. "What's that supposed to mean?"

"Oh. Sorry."

"I've worked like a maniac to get where I am. All of this—" he swept his hand through the air. "—it's because of *hard work*. And my drive to succeed. And my passion for my purpose in life. It's in my blood."

"I know."

"Do you like my place?"

"Yes."

"Good. I like it too. I love this place more than I love my mother. The things you see in here—in the basement floor, in the parlor, in the third floor, in here—I selected all that you see with *intention*. See that Morris?" He pointed at some colorful shapes on a canvas.

"Yeah?"

"I bought that because—"

"Wait. Sorry. George L. K. Morris?"

"Yes."

"That's an original?"

"See? That's what I'm *saying*. Everything in my home is chosen with *intention*."

"That's impressive. What do your folks think of your place?"

Harry exhaled. "My father's proud. If there's one thing I know, it's that my father is proud of me. I know Father is proud of me. My sister loves this place. I mean, she sees it on FaceTime."

"Has your sister been here?"

"Once. Yeah, she's impressed with my place. Her place is nice too. My mother—well, obviously. She loves my place more than I do. She thinks she lives here." Harry laughed. "The problem is that Mother thinks Steven lives here. Yeah, my younger brother. I mean, I told her, he's welcome to stay, as long as he asks me at least three months in advance. I don't think that's too much to ask. Do you? No, me neither. I mean, technically I own four apartments, so it's not too much trouble. So long as he asks me at least three months in advance. But anyway. As of Thursday, the basement level is occupied."

I stared.

Harry sighed. "Yeah, Steven's here on Thursday."

I couldn't stop myself: "That's okay, isn't it?"

"Yeah, technically it's one of four apartments. So yeah, no problem." Harry blew. "No problem."

"I love your place, Harry."

"Do you? Because it seemed like you might have been uncomfortable."

"I just need some time."

"Is it too warm for you?"

I snorted. "No. It's just…"

"A *little* too warm?"

"It's… decadent."

"Oh. But you're used to that?"

Eye contact.

"Well, I—"

"You belong here, Rachael."

Eyes locked.

"I do?"

"Yes."

Woah. What did that mean?

"You said you like my place."

"I did."

"Well then."

Crystalline eyes.

"Come closer."

I wriggled closer. Our knees connected.

"Did you enjoy dinner?"

"Yes."

"What about the car ride?"

"Yeah. That was good."

"She's brand new."

"I just liked the drive through Central Park."

"Me too." Clive Christian and pears emanated. Harry lifted his muscular arms. I let him squeeze my shoulders.

"Do you enjoy this?"

My arms were warm where he massaged.

"Yes."

"Do you like me?"

I looked away.

"Rachael."

The arm massage was an odd move. And yet...

I liked it.

I dived back into his sky eyes.

"Do you like me?"

The answer was:

"Yes."

"Rachael—I love you."

"I love everything."

Chapter 12

Harry froze. He still held my arms. He stared.

"What?"

"I love everything."

"You love everything."

"I love *you*. That includes *you*."

"Um..." Harry stared. "What?"

"I love you too."

"I just told you that I—something—you."

"And I just told you that I love you too."

His heavy, strong fingers squeezed my arm. It felt so good.

"What do you mean by—"

"I don't know? I just said it."

Harry puffed. "Are you aware that it's very difficult for me to say what I just said?"

"Of course, Harry. That's normal." *I was not normal.* "I love you too, Harry."

He shook his gold head, still squeezing my arm. "Are you—sure?"

"I'm sure."

"You haven't known me very long."

"One month and three weeks and four days."

"How do you know that?"

"Because I do."

Harry seemed to tremble. "I meant what I said."

"Me too."

"But—"

"Harry. Kiss me."

Surprised eyes.

I pouted.

Harry kissed me!

"There."

"Rachael—"

"Yes?"

"I don't understand you."

"That was good though, wasn't it?"

Harry hesitated. "Yeah. Can we do it again?"

I smiled. Nodded.

We kissed again!

"Okay, I believe you now."

"Good!"

Harry laughed. He let go of my arm, but our knees stayed connected.

"Did you mean what you said?"

"Yes."

"No. I mean—the other thing."

"What was that?"

"You said, 'I love everything.'"

I made a face. "Oh. Yeah."

"What do you mean by that?"

"I mean that I love everything."

"Okay, but—"

"Let's just forget it."

Harry looked awfully serious. Once again.

"C'mon."

The rest of the night was perfect. We didn't talk about love. There was no need.

Yet Harry *thought*. I knew all about thinking.

Daylight came. And I knew Harry *thought*. As I went about my day, I didn't think. I texted everyone except Sage about Harry. I texted Sage about everything except Harry! I cleaned my apartment. I drank some apple juice. I played fetch with Victory in my little living room. They taught me how to not think. Work loomed, and I remembered joy: Harry!

I even texted with him. Clearly, I'd upset him. Yet that wasn't what he texted about. In his words—I'm not kidding—I was "fascinating." I made him "feel" like he hadn't "felt before." Predictably, I was "beautiful." A "goddess," in fact. Apparently, I was even "astonishing!"

"I love you," Harry texted me. And though Harry didn't mention it, I knew that he thought and thought about what I'd said. About loving everything. That was okay! I knew that Harry thought happy thoughts. And I knew that he would be okay! Now I knew something else, too: Harry was infinitely wonderful. I loved Harry, too.

Only—*Xavier*! Oh no, what was I going to do? *What was I going to do*? Was I meant to tell Xavier what happened? Was I meant to tell Xavier about Harry?

It got late. I covered my face with my hand. Lay on my soft, violet bed. Victory scampered across the ash carpet. I peeked through my fingers. I watched Victory scratch my bedroom's poor little corner. Months ago, they'd damaged it beyond repair. Insulation sprayed over the patchy carpet. I'd used increasingly creative techniques to hide the truth from my landlord. He would never know.

I closed my eyes.

Likewise, Xavier would never know about Harry.

Darkness.

I opened my eyes. Hours had passed. I didn't know how many. I smelled something. Victory had let themself go in the living room again. I groaned. I'd deal with it later. I didn't feel good. I needed to be at work soon. Not even by choice.

But what was the point in work? I used to have so much respect for the Volcker Rule's naming origin. I still did!—yet somehow, my office had almost made me hate him. I just didn't understand *why* I'd go to work in a few hours. I'd rode that train a thousand times. I'd sat in that cubicle a thousand and one! *Why?*

I wanted to call Sage. But my iPhone said it was past midnight. Surely Sage was asleep.

I heard Victory sigh from the living room. Normally, Victory made me happy! But they'd let themself go on the living room carpet. Right now, not even Victory made me smile.

How much longer would I work for Citigroup?

How much longer would I live?

I watched my room, contemplating it:

Time.

A half-glass of apple juice still stood on my wooden bedside table. But by now, the juice must have warmed. The yellow hyacinths danced in their vase. But in two weeks, those bright flowers would be gone—and in one year, that fragrant plant would be gone. My little ceiling had shining lights. My seat was plush brown in the corner. My violet sheets were warm and comforting. Yet in two years, this bedroom would be unrecognizable—and in five years, that calm wallpaper would peel. In ten years, my own face would wrinkle! In 15 years, Victory would be gone. In 50 years, my favorite mother and my beloved father would be gone. In 80 years—only 80 years!—Isabel would be gone. Devonte would be gone. Sage would be gone. I would be gone.

And time wouldn't stop. Time would tear down this entire apartment block. We'd build something new. Then time would tear that down too!

I shivered. Switched off the lights. Sat under the covers, hugged my knees. Tears filled my eyes. I looked out the window. New York City was heartachingly dazzling at night. Yet in two hundred years, how would this cityscape look? What about one thousand?

And one thousand years was *nothing*.

Five thousand years from now:

Where would my parents be? They had to be *somewhere*. Where would Sage be? She had to be *somewhere*! What about me? Five thousand years from now, would my City even exist?

Time was perceptual. These seemed like long amounts of time, right? But they *weren't*. I'd existed for maybe 27 years. We'd existed for maybe 300,000. The universe had existed for maybe 13,800,000,000. It might exist for another 100,000,000,000,000. And then—

That was it.

What the hell was ten thousand years?

Yet in only ten thousand years, everything I saw would literally crumble into dust.

And in only a hundred trillion years, time would literally sweep our universe away.

Right before my eyes.

Everything disintegrated.

I gazed out my window.

Through my falling tears.

I gazed until—

At last—

I stopped feeling sad.

Because the sounds of the City were music to my ears. And now the image in my bedroom window made me cry with joy. Headlights, streetlights, skyscrapers, tiny windows. Blinking in darkness. And gently glowing within... quiet reflections. My night light. My violet bed. My shining face. My soaking hair.

Eye contact.

I smiled!

How could I have forgotten the infinite solution?

Time didn't exist in eye contact.

I smiled at myself in the window!

I loved myself.

Sobbed.

Laughed at everything.

Snuffled.

Laughed at myself!

Time didn't stand a chance.

Chapter 13

Sage told me what happened next.

All the City's parks bloomed, and one evening, Sage walked in State Street. She caught up on *The Read* as the sun set, looking forward to winding down at home. Until she saw a shape. She looked into The Battery. A well-dressed male hid in a shrub!

Sage was startled.

She stopped in the street. Peered a little closer. She thought she recognized that hulking man in the shrub! But she couldn't be *sure*. So she paused her podcast, removed an AirPod, and tiptoed into the park.

Suddenly, she gasped!

There was no question.

Harry Davis hid in the shrub!

Sage wanted to go home. But her Lower East Side apartment wasn't far, and now she was amused—and curious. Why would one of her wealthiest acquaintances hide in a flourishing shrub in The Battery? Wearing a custom-tailored suit worth more than her car?

Well, Sage clarified, Harry may not have been *in* the shrub. He may have stood *behind* the shrub. Or—*through* the shrub? *Under* the shrub? The specifics were unclear.

Yet Sage told me this was definitely Harry Davis. And definitely an expensive suit.

The Battery bathed in amber sunlight. People gazed at plaques and monuments. Ordered from food trucks. Ambled around. Hands in pockets, Sage stood near State Street. She was ready to continue home. Until she noticed the blond hair in the distance. And it seemed that Harry watched the blond hair! Whoever owned it walked with someone. Sage squinted.

No.

Could it be?

Was Harry looking at *me*?

Now, Sage couldn't leave the park. She was transfixed.

Sage's first instinct was to call me. But if she looked at *me* in the distance, I was clearly *with* someone. Elegant. Somewhat taller. Inky-black hair. Slender. If she really looked at *me*, surely *now* was not the time to call?

Countless thoughts rushed through Sage's mind:

Is that Rachael?

Who is that she's with?

Why is Harry watching them?

That's definitely *Harry.*

He's going to ruin his suit!

This is none of my business.

But I'm sick of minding my own business.

I'd rather watch this than think about work.

Abigail was horrific today.

I want to go home!

I need some of that Bravado hot sauce.

Should I eat it with the fish?

I could just squeeze it into my mouth.

I need to go.

But Rachael is safe—right?

Wait—is that even Rachael?

Sage stepped through the grass.

She opened her mouth—

But Harry whispered to himself!

"I get it."

Sage froze behind a planetree. She stood several feet from Harry's shrub. He hadn't noticed her. Yet Sage heard his whispers clearly:

"You told me. You love me. You told me."

Sage couldn't believe her ears!

"But I get it. You love *everything*. I totally understand. You have such a gigantic heart."

Sage covered her mouth.

"You love him. It's clear! The whole park can see! Because you love *everything*. Well, you know what, Rachael? *I* love everything too. I understand you now. I love you. And you love me. But you love *everything*. Well, you know what? *I love everything too.*"

A twig snapped under Sage's boot.

Harry's head rotated!

Sage covered her mouth.

Obscured by the planetree, her heart raced!

Seconds stretched.

Sage didn't breathe.

Harry resumed.

"I love you, Rachael. You said that you love me too. I believe you. I love everything. Just like you. I bet *he* doesn't love everything. He doesn't even know you! *I* do. I know that you love everything. *He's* not on our level. He doesn't understand loving everything. Not like us."

Sage was immobilized!

"He doesn't know the *first thing* about you. Why would you even go for a Chinese? Well, I guess it makes sense. You love *everything*. No, I understand. I love everything too. That silly man doesn't stand a chance. Everyone in this park can see you love him. They should know he doesn't stand a chance! We're going to be together, Rachael. It's prearranged. We're meant to be together. You taught me how to love everything. It's just a matter of time."

Sage had heard more than enough! Stealthily, she slipped away. Back on State Street, she called me.

*

I was with Xavier, and ignored the buzzing in my pocket.

Because it was true! Xavier had taken me to The Battery. Spring warmed, and we had a lovely time. The next day, on my lunch break, I called Sage back.

"*Oh* my gosh."

"Hi."

"Rachael. What are you doing?"

"I'm sorry. I've been busy."

"I called you five times."

"At least eight."

"You don't text!?"

"Sage, I'm sorry."

"Well obviously you didn't read my messages. I need to tell you something!"

Sage filled me in. About Harry in the shrub. *Under* the shrub. *Through* the shrub? Whatever it was—Sage filled me in!

"He's insane."

"He's a lot."

"He's *out of his mind*."

"I mean, he's a lot. He's not crazy."

"Rachael—"

"As soon as you introduced us, I saw he was a lot."

"You're kidding me."

"I don't think he's crazy."

"He's going to *kill* you!"

I laughed. "No he's not!"

"You still haven't told me who that Chinese guy was!"

"I will. I'll tell you."

"He was hot."

"Sage. He's hotter than Harry."

"So why the hell are you still seeing Harry?"

"I love him."

"*Unbelievable!*"

"I do!"

"No, you don't."

"Sage, I love him."

"*Really?*"

"I think so. He's so much nicer than you think."

"I mean, I think he's nice. I just think he's kind of a—"

"A what?"

"He's a WASP. He's whiteness personified!"

"I know that."

"So why are you still seeing him?"

"Why did you introduce him to me?"

"I thought you could be a good match. But I didn't know him that well. I didn't realize how square he is. When I introduced you, I saw it. He's clueless. He's white-shoe. I mean, if you just want money, go for it. But you're so much better."

"Am I, though?"

"*Yes*! At least, I want you to be. Which school did he go to?"

"Pri—"

"Princeton! See, I didn't even need to ask. He's not even a good person."

"He is! You don't know him. He's really sweet!"

"Are you sure?"

"Yes. He's a sweetheart."

"Why didn't you tell me about that other guy?"

"I wasn't ready."

"Tell me about him."

"He's—"

Sage waited.

"He's even more amazing. He's—I can't explain it."

"You like him more than Harry?"

"I—I don't know. But—"

"So, go for him!"

"*Maybe*."

"What's his name?"

"I don't wanna tell you."

"Oh, c'mon."

"I can tell you *about* him."

"Okay, don't tell me his name. Tell me *about* him."

"I mean, I can *try* to tell you about him. He's not like Harry. He's not like anyone. He—Oh, where do I start?"

"Start at the start. Where did you meet?"

"Times Square."

"Times Square?"

"See, this is why I didn't want to tell you."

"Rachael, tell me whatever you want to tell me."

"Isn't that what I'm doing? Okay. So we met, and then—see, I don't even know what to say. We connected. Like—straight away. Like it was all supposed to happen. I don't know if it was a higher power or if it was because it was *between 3:30 p.m. and 5:10 p.m.* or, what. It might have been after 5:10 p.m., that's why I don't know."

"Our lucky time is between 11:30 a.m. and 12:30 p.m."

"Every Virgo is different. Like, *yes*, but it's also between 3:30 p.m and 5:10 p.m. But we might have met just *after* 5:10 p.m., is what I'm saying."

"Is he a Capricorn?"

"No."

"Scorpio?"

"No. He's not even a Cancer or a Taurus."

"What is he?"

"He's a Gemini."

Sage burst out laughing.

"There's no explanation for it. We just—"

"You gelled."

"We gelled! We connected. And he's not like anyone I've ever met. He's—he's quiet. It takes him time to let people in."

"Is he Chinese?"

"Yes! And he grew up in this apartment building in Chinatown, like, several generations of his family have lived in the same building for like more than a hundred years. I haven't seen it. But he's a New Yorker. And he's, like, *contained*. Like, he's not shy. He's a male model. He's a professional male model for Louis Vuitton. But, it's hard to be an Asian male model. It's hard to be Asian, full stop. But his agency is really good. He's with multiple agencies. And he's got a massive Instagram following, like, more than 100K followers. And he's rich. Obviously. But, not like Harry. He has more money than we do. And he's so kind, like really really kind, and I think he really likes me. And I feel the same way. It's like I don't even get to choose. It's all predetermined. I'm supposed to see both of them. But Xavier is—oh, shoot. No, I don't know anyone called Xavier. But this guy, this Chinese guy, he's more intellectual than he seems. He's laser-sharp. He goes to entertainment centers, and he wins. I mean, he *wins*. Blackjack and that Chinese game, Ma—what's it called? Mahjong, yeah. He's brilliant. Like, so talented. And he has at least two sisters, and a brother, and he's—Why are we talking about men!?"

Sage exploded with laughter.

"What's so funny?"

"Are you in the Ladies'?"

"Yeah, I'm on lunch break."

"Okay, babe, you gotta get back to work."

"But you started me!"

"I just want to warn you about Harry. He's insane. I saw him, he was talking to himself! Shaking, and spluttering. He's obsessed with you, Rachael."

"Thank you for telling me."

"Don't dismiss me! He might be dangerous."

"He's not dangerous."

"He hates Xavier. I know that's his name. He might try and assassinate him, or something."

"Whoa, Sage!"

"I'm being serious. And he was talking about 'I love everything,' and all this other nonsense. And he's racist. Don't you remember when I brought up China at that party? When I introduced you. He thinks he runs the world."

"I mean, he kinda *does*."

"Rachael, stay away from Harry. That's all I'm saying."

"Okay, I hear you."

"Good. Hear me."

"I do."

"Anyway, I'm happy for you. Xavier sounds nice."

Chapter 14

Sage was right. Xavier was nice!

Even my dad said so. My dad was hard to please! But even my dad liked Xavier.

It was awkward when they met. It happened accidentally. It was my mom's fault!

I went to Trader Joe's with Xavier, for some reason. I'd always loved Trader Joe's. Xavier liked it too. We picked out some snacks only Trader Joe's would stock. Brown Sugar Boba Mochi, and Pumpkin Spice Espresso Beans. Rosemary Croissant Croutons, which I wanted to eat on their own. It was late afternoon—the checkout line stretched around the store's perimeter. Patiently, we stood in line. And I heard Mom's voice!

Oh no!

"Hold this." I pushed my groceries into Xavier's arms.

"Oh, sure." He was so obedient.

I walked off—

"Baby?"

Only Mom called me that.

I kept walking.

"Rachael!"

I stopped.

"Baby, come here. We haven't seen you for ages."

I loved my parents. I couldn't ignore them!

"Now's not a good time."

"Oh, stop it. The grocery store is totally appropriate!"

I turned. "Hi."

Several heads turned. Xavier looked from my parents to me. He was confused.

"Come here, Rachael."

"Mom, it's not a good time!"

"We've missed you. How are you? How's Victory?" Mom's beady eyes were huge behind her thick glasses. Concerned.

"They're good. I'm good. Can we catch up later?"

My dad stood behind her. Dirty flannel shirt. Arms crossed. "Joanne, she's busy."

"I don't know what all this fuss is about." Mom tried hugging me!

I relented. "Hi Mom." We hugged. I rubbed her back, for some reason.

"*That's* more like it. We love you. Now give your father a hug."

My parents would never change!

Xavier stared intensely at the bottled water shelf. I tried not to look at him. But it was impossible.

"And who—"

I froze.

"Oh, my name's Xavier."

"Xavier, good to meet you!" Mom beamed at Xavier. Waved.

Xavier waved back.

My dad moved with the awkwardness of a sea creature.

Right before my eyes, Xavier and my dad shook hands!

I couldn't believe this!

"Well, now I can see why you didn't wanna say 'Hi!'" Mom cackled.

I died a little, inside.

"Joanne, I really think we should get going." Dad scratched his head.

"Not so fast!" Mom enjoyed this. "Is Xavier special?"

"Mom, you can't be serious!"

Xavier spoke softly. "Rachael and I just met."

"Uhuh." Mom's eyes were like satellites. "And you're already shopping together?"

"Joanne—"

Mom eyed Xavier. "Well, as long as you're having fun."

"*Enough*, Mom. I'll call you later."

"You *better*, baby. Good catch, by the way." Mom winked.

I scowled at her! Dad loudly cleared his throat. Xavier laughed.

"Nice to meet you," Xavier said.

"And you too." My dad approved.

"Rachael, don't get ahead of yourself, now." Mom wagged a finger. "Actually, where are you two headed after this?"

"Now. Is. Not. The. Time!" I fumed. People watched us.

"Jeez, relax, baby." Mom still thought this was funny. "You two take care now. It's my pleasure to meet you, Xavier."

"You too."

"Would you stop encouraging them?" I told Xavier.

"Careful." Mom turned. "My baby bites."

I put my face in my hands.

My parents disappeared into the aisle.

"You bite?" Xavier asked.

"No, obviously not. God, I hate her."

"Your mom seems really lovely." Xavier's eyebrows raised. "She's really funny." Xavier tried not to laugh. He was amused.

"Well, she's not. Why did you act all nice to them?"

"What do you mean? I'm a nice guy." Xavier's lips fell. "I'm nice to people. You know that. And that was mean of you. To your parents. They probably haven't seen you for a while. They just want to know you're okay."

"Stop saying obvious things."

"Rachael, you're normally so nice. One of the nicest people I've met. You're so kind. You love people. Wouldn't you extend that courtesy to your parents? You love them. Don't be embarrassed because they met me."

"I just wasn't ready for that."

"I mean, neither was I." Our line turned the corner. "But I'm good at faking it."

"My dad likes you."

"How do you know?"

"I know my dad. He's not easy to win over. But you already have."

"I'm blessed." Xavier's infinite eyes sparkled. "Your parents seem nice."

I watched Xavier as we neared the register. He didn't look at his iPhone. He looked straight ahead. His eyes were even. *He* was even. His jaw was clean. It didn't twitch. He was so *composed*. He knew I watched him. He let me watch him. He knew I liked it. His hands were in his Abercrombie & Fitch pockets. He had it *together*. He was at peace with himself. Whether or not he met my parents didn't bother him. I mean, it *mattered* to him. But I saw that he was okay either way. He *flowed*. For Xavier, the world came, and the world went. Xavier was water. And of the four elements, water was the strongest. Xavier knew that.

"How long are you going to let me look at you?"

"Until we gotta pay."

"What if I want to keep looking at you when we're paying?"

"That would be okay too."

"But you're paying, right?"

"Sure."

"I'm joking." Lightly I slapped him. "We always go halves."

"You know I can pay right?"

"Yes. But I choose to."

"Okay."

"I mean, I picked the croutons. And also the mochi and the dried mango."

"You're trying to pay for all of it, right?"

Lightly I pushed him. "Halves."

"Okay."

"Next in line!"

Chapter 15

I really liked him. I knew it even before we met! I thought about him when I was a kid. In elementary school, I'd envisioned him differently. More heroic. Less gentle. More engaged. Less attractive. Yet I knew this was the same person. I can't explain how. I just did.

I never thought my first boyfriend was him. Samuel was my first boyfriend. I liked him a lot. We were just so young, and I always knew I'd meet more people. I think Samuel knew the same thing. There was a time, though, when I thought my first girlfriend was him. Actually, it was an entire period of time. Her name was Tiana. I was in my early twenties, and Tiana was a few years older. We could have been together for way longer. But I ended it after two years, and we stayed friends. And then there was my most recent ex. I don't want to say his name, and I don't want to tell you the whole story. But I want to tell you that I thought he was the man I'd imagined as a kid too. Only briefly. Pretty quickly, I realized I was wrong.

Xavier wasn't like anyone I'd met. He was deeply kind. He loved his family. His mother's Christian name was Carla, and his father's was George. Xavier's parents owned a grocery store in Chinatown. All five of the Pang children had worked there. Nowadays Xavier's older sister, Angela, worked as a lawyer in Washington D.C. Xavier's brother worked in tech. The younger siblings still went to school: one Upstate, and the other in California. Xavier and Angela brought in most of the family's money.

But Xavier wasn't always kind. He had a streak. Sometimes I wished he didn't have that streak. But other times I accepted it. Xavier liked certain things. Blackjack, for example. I wished he would give it up. But he loved it. Why should he stop doing something he loved?

Xavier was an uncomplicated person. Yet he was deep. I'm going to do my best to explain it. Xavier was not a thinker. He was almost always calm. He let the world pass him by. He enjoyed smelling the roses. But Xavier was competitive. He told me there were very few Asian male models in New York. At first, I found this hard to believe. But eventually I realized Xavier didn't claim to be one of the only Asian male models in New York. He was too modest to say what he really meant. Very few of New York's Asian male models were *as successful as Xavier.* When I figured this out, I asked him how he'd made it. And as usual, he replied in riddles:

"I do my job."

"What do you mean, you do your job?"

"I *do* it."

He spoke a certain way. By 'I do my job,' Xavier meant: 'I work harder than anyone else.'

And Xavier was wise. He knew certain things. Universal truths. Things he had no business knowing. Sometimes I even thought Xavier had magical abilities. Once, we were in Central Park. And I lost my lipstick. I stood to search for it. But Xavier spoke my name. He pointed in the grass. It had taken him less than a second to find my lipstick!

Money made the world go round. And I accepted the world—I loved it! But sometimes I couldn't believe I'd ended up at Citibank. As far as my work was concerned, the only thing of any significance was money. And I worked for those who had too much—meanwhile, the world overflowed with those who didn't have enough. Why did I do it? Well, I didn't have the answer. But *the way I felt when I was with Xavier*—that was pretty close. And I was sure of one thing. The way I felt when I was with Xavier had nothing to do with money.

What I did felt right. I made time for Xavier *and* Harry. Sometimes I felt guilty. But most of the time, I felt good. It was too early to exclude anyone. Xavier didn't know about Harry. But he understood I didn't want to be serious. We talked about it. I think he understood me. But Harry was a whole different story.

I tried not to tell Harry Sage had seen him in the shrub. *On* the shrub. *Throughout* the shrub? I tried not to tell

Harry. But I only lasted a few days. Of course I had to tell him. The story was ludicrous, after all.

"Who's the lucky man, then?" Harry sat across another white tablecloth.

"His name's Xavier."

Heat reddened his face. "Did you think about telling me?"

"Yes."

"Why didn't you?"

"I was going to."

"And how did you expect me to react?"

"I knew you'd be upset."

"Well, you were wrong! I'm not upset." Now his face was purple. "No way, José. Not upset."

"No?"

"Nope. Not even a little bit. I'm not upset."

"Well, that's good."

"I'm not."

"I know."

"I'm not upset. But you could have told me."

"I was just about to."

"But how long were you—"

"How long were you spying on me?"

Harry choked on his asparagus. "Do you think I was— *spying* on you?"

"I know you were."

Harry breathed liked a rhinoceros. "*Spying*!"

"Is there a better term?"

"I wasn't *spying*! I just *saw you* in the park—"

"You always talk to yourself when you recognize someone in public?"

"*Rachael*!" The Michelin Star restaurant went quiet. "*You think I just recognized—'Someone*!?'"

I felt guilty. "You recognized me."

His eyes bulged. "*Do you have any idea how much I care about you*!?"

Several emotions mixed. "I'm sorry."

Harry huffed. Harry puffed. Harry swallowed his asparagus. The Michelin Star restaurant resumed its dignified chatter.

Following the shrub incident, Sage and Harry became sworn enemies. Sage accepted me no matter what I did. Just as I accepted Sage, no matter what Sage did. We had always been this way. But this didn't mean Sage and I actively supported each and every decision made by the other. It didn't matter how much Sage loved *Bridgerton*. I was never going to watch it. In the same way, it didn't matter how much I loved Harry. Sage was never going to want us to be together.

Harry didn't much like Sage, either.

But Sage seemed to like Xavier. They hadn't met. I *really* wanted to keep it that way. But I knew that Sage liked the idea of Xavier with me. She knew I didn't want to talk about him. She really tried not to bring up the topic. But I knew her so well. Whenever she imagined Xavier with me, she walked around with this *inner smile*. I pretended not to notice it. But we knew each other too well. I knew that one day, I was going to feel that inner smile, too. It would be because Sage had found her person.

Chapter 16

Now Harry knew about Xavier.

But Xavier didn't know about Harry.

"You know that I like you, right?"

We were somewhere in The Bronx. Walking by a busy shopping strip. Sometimes when we walked, I lost track of our location—even without today's mist.

"Yes. Sure."

"I really like you."

"You just said that."

"Is everything okay?"

"Yes. Why?"

"I'm just making sure."

"I'm good." Xavier wore a beige Oscar Jacobson overshirt. Green Burberry shades. Something caught his attention. "That's cute." It was a meowing tabby cat. "Are you having a nice day?" Xavier bent down to stroke her. "You're so nice." She peeked up at him.

Xavier was so interesting.

The tabby stretched in her filthy corner. "Say 'Hello' to Rachael." She was covered in spiderwebs and what looked like sand.

"Hi!" I wasn't sure I wanted to touch her. So I waved.

Then she made eye contact with me. So I bent.

I stroked her fur.

I also stroked Xavier's hand.

"Isn't it nice?" Xavier said.

"It's a 'she.'"

"Yes."

"She's nice."

The cat and our hands formed a warm ball of delight. And also some spiderwebs and sand.

"Did I tell you I have a cat?"

"You didn't. Did I tell you I have a puppy?"

"Is that a question? I feel like me and Victory already see eye-to-eye on certain topics."

I laughed. "You haven't even met."

"We may as well have met."

We continued down the street. "Am I boring?"

"You talk about Victory a lot."

"Do I?"

"It's okay though."

"What's your cat's name?"

"Ruby."

"Ruby!"

"Yeah."

"That's so beautiful!"

"It is?"

"Yes! Is she a girl?"

"Yes."

"What type of kitty is she?"

"Burmese."

"What color?"

"I don't know."

"What do you mean, you don't know?"

"Basically black."

"Okay. Why didn't you tell me about her before?"

"I don't know. I don't tell many people about her."

"Oh." Suddenly, his words made me feel a certain way. "Okay."

"But I just told you about her."

"Well, thanks." The mood had shifted. People yelled at one another across the street. We passed them before we spoke again. "She sounds like a nice cat."

"She's just a cat."

Feelings clashed inside me. I didn't understand some of them. Why was I angry?

"You want to go in here?" Xavier pointed into a deli.

"Not really."

Xavier stopped outside. His mouth opened—

—But I spoke first. "Just go in."

He raised an eyebrow.

I followed him inside.

He narrowed his eyes at the coffee machine.

I stood near the door.

His hands were in his chinos pockets. He looked at me.

"Are you getting anything?" I asked.

He only looked at me.

"Well?"

"I don't know." He disappeared behind a shelf.

I crossed my arms and stayed by the entrance.

Xavier slipped into vision. "Look at this." He held a pink packet of Smoothies Skittles.

I looked away.

"Think I should get it?"

"I don't care."

Xavier stared at me.

I glared back.

"What's wrong?"

"Nothing!"

Someone yelled outside. I couldn't understand his words. He crashed into the corner store. Berated the middle-aged man behind the curved glass display.

Xavier watched me. Everyone else looked at the yeller.

"That's why I told you! You gotta do me right! I swear to God!"

The middle-aged man was unfazed. "I *do* you right."

"Nah, don't play with me!"

Behind the yeller's back, I slipped out of the corner store. Xavier followed.

We continued under the train track.

"Did you want me to head home?" He spoke quietly.

"I don't know. Did you even see what happened in there?"

"Ah, you mean that guy?"

"Let's find a nice area. You didn't even look at what was happening."

"Obviously I noticed that guy. So, you *don't* want me to go home?"

"I just said I want to find a nice area. Why are you so annoying?"

"What are you talking about?"

"I don't know."

"Well, if you think I'm annoying, we don't have to hang out."

"I just want to find a good spot. This place freaks me out. Do you think that man is okay though?"

"That crazy guy?"

"Yeah, do you think he's okay?"

"Ah—yes?"

"What about the owner of the shop?"

"I'm sure it's fine."

"Are you comfortable here?

"I am. But let's find somewhere nicer."

"Honestly, this place isn't that bad."

Xavier clicked his tongue. "Okay. Follow me."

"Yes, Sir." I followed him. "Where you gonna take me? Wendy's?"

"There's a nice park here."

"Oh, Van Cortlandt?"

"Probably."

"It's Van Cortlandt."

"You're very intelligent."

"You suck."

"What's wrong with you today?"

"I'm in a bad mood."

"Are you sure you want to hang out?"

"Xavier, if you ask me that one more time, the answer just might change."

I didn't know why I was upset. But Xavier's patience wore thin. I knew it.

"Why didn't you tell me about your cat?"

"Is *that* why you're in a bad mood?"

"Just answer the question."

Xavier paused. "I told you, I don't talk about her much."

"She's just a cat, right?"

Xavier stared at me through his designer shades.

I changed my mind. "I don't want to talk about it. Let's just walk in the park. I'm sorry I'm weird."

"You're not weird." Xavier often told me I wasn't weird. This was why I liked him.

"You've been here before, right?" Van Cortlandt Park surrounded us, and together, we walked down its path.

"Yeah."

"What was it like growing up in Chinatown?"

"I think we gotta talk."

"I don't wanna."

"What was your last boyfriend like?"

I couldn't believe my ears! "Um... Are you sure you wanna go there?"

"Yes."

Van Cortlandt Park was nice, but some of the grass was brown.

"Can you ask a different question?"

"Sure." Xavier thought. "What is it like to love everything?"

Xavier was something else!

"You know what? That's a good question."

Xavier watched the side of my face. Tried to figure me out.

"I'm not being sarcastic. I'll tell you." I smiled at him. "It's a good question. I've always loved everything. And when I was younger, I actually *decided* that I love everything. That's probably what made the difference."

"Interesting."

"That's my least favorite compliment."

Xavier was silent.

"I've told you before. Please don't call me interesting."

"I didn't call you interesting. I just said, 'Interesting.'"

"Fine. Do you think *I'm* interesting?"

He hesitated. "...No."

"Yay!"

Xavier laughed.

"I'm not interesting. I just love everything. It's just how I am."

"Wow." Xavier contemplated. "I don't love everything. I can't imagine what that's like. But—does it mean you don't want an exclusive relationship?"

My breath caught in my throat. I opened my mouth—

"Sorry for the question."

"I—"

"Have you actually had one?"

And I tripped on a little grass tuft! Flailed my arms. Tried not to fall—

But Xavier's strong arms were around me.

He held me on the path. My heart beat so fast. His breath was warm on the side of my neck.

"Thank you."

"No problem."

His arms relaxed around my body. He was about to let go—

"Thanks Xavier."

But the moment was over. His hands were in his pockets.

I took a giant step along the path. Like nothing had happened. "The answer is... yes."

Xavier walked to my right. Hands in pockets.

"I've had about three relationships."

"I know that."

"I mean, three serious ones."

"Three exclusive ones?"

I bit my lip. Inhaled. "Yes."

"What was it like?"

Sometimes, it was like he knew me better than I did. Xavier was sensitive. Emotionally intelligent. He knew that right now, I *wanted* to answer these questions.

"Good. It was good."

"Tell me about them."

Today, the sun was bright. I closed my eyes. "Okay." I opened my eyes. Our path extended ahead. "Wait. What do you wanna know?"

"Tell me about your first relationship."

"You've gotta tell me about yours after."

"Sure."

"Okay. My first boyfriend's name was... Samuel. That was good. I think we were pretty compatible. He was a Scorpio. He was one grade above me."

"He went to your high school?"

"Yes. And he was *okay*. But I was like... a completely different person back then."

"Did you love everything at this time?"

I burst out laughing. "Um—well yeah, I told you! I always have."

"But, what I mean is, was this before or after you *decided* that you loved everything?"

I frowned. "Um... okay, next question."

Xavier clicked his tongue. "Alright. How did it end?"

"He graduated high school."

"You didn't keep in touch?"

"I mean, he wanted to."

"You ended it."

"I've ended all of my relationships."

Xavier was quiet. "All of them?"

"Yes."

"Me too."

"Really?"

"Yes. Every time."

"How many relationships have you had?"

We walked slowly.

Xavier ran a finger through his soft hair. "Depends what you mean."

"You know what I mean. Serious ones."

"It still depends what you mean."

"I'm asking you the same question you asked me." I laughed. "It's not complicated."

"So—Hm. Maybe, between one and..."

I looked at him.

"...more."

"So, a minimum of one, right?"

Xavier nodded.

"So your ex was more serious than every other relationship you've had."

"Yeah." Xavier looked ahead.

"The one you told me about."

"I think so."

"Cora."

"Yes."

"You were monogamous?"

"Obviously. Yes."

"How long were you together?"

"Almost two years."

"When did you leave her?"

"I didn't leave her. But we broke up in 2020."

"2020. Four years ago. But what do you mean, you didn't leave her?"

"It's more complicated than that."

"So, what happened?"

He opened his slender hands. "We broke up."

"Didn't you just say you ended all of your relationships?"

"I guess we broke up because of me."

"So, you ended the relationship?"

"Ye—No."

"Okay. So the relationship ended *because* of you."

"Maybe that's more accurate."

"Wait." Oh no. "So you *didn't* end the relationship?" Was this a red flag?

"I—kind of did."

"Please elaborate."

But Xavier was calm. "The relationship ended because of me. I guess I probably ended it."

I stamped my foot on the path. "Xavier, *did* you or *did you not* end your last relationship?"

"My last relationship?"

"The one—" My temper rose again. "The one with Cora! The relationship we're talking about. *Why* is this so hard?"

Xavier cleared his throat. "You know what, I'll just tell you. Cora and I broke up in 2020. We had issues. I'm happy to tell you about them. Basically, we were together for two years. We had a professional relationship, but we— we fell in love. But it was never going to be for*ever*. Cora was a model. I told you that. She still is a model. Yeah, we lived together. The whole thing. I'm not really a 'relationship person.' But I've had relationships. Cora was the strongest. The most 'serious,' if that's what you want to call it. But it was never going to be forever. She—Cora— I guess she wanted it to be forever. I tried to be honest with her. Anyway, it was a good relationship. But it was always going to end. All things must pass. I know that you know that, in your own way. The brightest flame burns the quickest. Now I sound like Instagram. I don't really care, anyway. But Cora and I were in love. We met after a shoot. It was so long ago. But we just—saw eye-to-eye. We treated each other as equals. And, you know. One thing leads to another, I guess. We were an item, which is rare in modeling. It lasted longer than anyone expected. We were together for a long time. It was a good experience, overall. Cora is—a good person. So, what do you want to know?"

I blinked tears. "I don't know. Why did you break up with her?" I sniffed.

"We don't have to talk about this."

"I want to."

"Are you sure?"

"Yes."

"Well—I didn't break up with her. We just—broke up. But maybe she wanted to continue. Actually, I've tried to forget all this. But you don't really get to choose your memories. I have a lot of good memories. We were really close. Anyway, we broke up. I made mistakes. I'm not proud of them."

Alarm bells! "What did you do?"

"No one is perfect. And Cora did the same thing."

"Stop."

Xavier looked at me.

"I don't want to hear it."

"I can just tell you."

"No." Whatever it was, I didn't want to know. "It's okay! Whatever you did, it's in the past."

"Rachael, I don't have any secrets."

"It's okay!" I smiled. "We've got time." I wiped my eyes.

"Rachael, if you ever want to know something, just ask."

"Yes. I will." The sun shone. "Anyway, I want to tell you about *me*."

Xavier laughed. "Go ahead."

"Am I that boring?"

"You are *not* boring."

"*Do not* say I'm interesting!"

Xavier zipped his lips shut with his fingers.

"Tell me about you later. But I want to tell you about me."

"Okay. But—do you think of me differently now?"

I definitely did. "No."

"Yes you do."

"No. Not really. You've made mistakes." I shrugged. I chose to believe Xavier had never cheated! On Cora, or on anyone! As long as it wasn't that, whatever he'd done was forgivable. "We're all human. I don't need to know right now."

"I'm not a bad person."

"I know that. You know what?" I surprised myself: "I know you're a good person."

"I'm not a saint."

"No one is."

"*You* are."

"I'm a saint?"

"You're a saint."

"Um—thank you?"

"Go. What do you want to tell me?"

"Same topic."

"Your relationships?"

"Yeah."

"Tell me about your relationships, then."

"They've been good. Um, you've gotta ask me a question."

"Okay. So, if you love everything, how do you balance that with being in an exclusive relationship?"

He was so specific. "—How long have you wanted to ask me this?"

"I don't know what you mean."

"*Fine*, Xavier. The answer is that I don't balance it. I love everyone. It's a problem. It's always been a problem. All of my relationships have been good. The last one was the worst one. He was a terrible person. But I sort of believe everyone is a good person. I know it doesn't make sense. Anyway, he was a terrible person. But the one before that—the serious one before that—it was with a woman. And that was really good. To be honest, we're still in touch. Now you know. But it's—we're just friends. I promise you. Sorry, you asked me a really specific question. So—it's hard for me to love one person. It feels natural, but also, *not*, at the same time. Part of me wants a monogamous relationship. I told you, all of my serious relationships have been monogamous. Exclusive. That's what you're asking, right?"

"Yes."

"I want monogamy. But in practice, it's hard. Probably my best relationship was with Tiana."

"Was that the serious one?"

"Yeah. I don't want to hurt your feelings. I just want to tell you, that was a really good relationship. I still love Tiana. I always will. We're just friends now, I promise you. But I have to tell you—That."

"That's okay."

"I mean, I love her as a friend."

"I know."

"You have to trust me on this!"

"I do."

"You're so amazing."

"I am?"

"Yes. You, Xavier. You're wonderful."

Xavier opened his mouth—

"You're perfect."

—"Thank you."

"You're a genuine, good person."

"Wah."

"You are!"

"You're flattering me." We walked on! Sunlight made all the little leaves look like emeralds, and a couple smiled at Xavier. At me. We smiled back! "I'm not a saint. But I try to be a good person. I'm happy."

"That's the most important thing!"

"It's important to be happy. Happiness is important. I need to know that my family are happy. I support my parents and my younger siblings. I do the things that I hope make people happy. I sort of hope that when people see me, they smile." I nodded, I knew exactly what Xavier meant! "My parents smile when we're together. To be honest, I miss them. We're doing some work this week, yeah, at the store. I'm really looking forward to it! One day—yeah, I think you'll meet them. I know, I met your parents! Haha, they are so lovely. Your mom seems like a nice woman. Yeah, I think your dad and I will get along too! I like your parents. One day you'll meet my family. They know about you. Haha, now you know! I told them.

Yes. They're funny people. Oh, the other day, my little brother—the tech one—so, his boyfriend gave my mom a postcard! His name's Mark. Mark is my brother's boyfriend. So, my mom's always loved Mark. My dad—he needs some time, you know. But my mom *loves* Mark, she gifts him our *candy* and *prayer lamps* and, *tea*—my mom is like that, you know. So the other day, Mark and my brother were at the store, and Mark gave Mom a postcard! Just a Philly postcard. He's from Philly. My mom likes postcards. She has a little collection. So Mark gave her this Philly postcard." Xavier stopped to show me the photograph. "Ah, Mom's funny. She loves it! See, they're already welcoming Mark into the family. Haha, but this one time, my dad asked Mark to speak more quietly! We were just talking, but like, to my dad's ears, Mark's voice is *loud*, you know? We just don't talk like that. It was so funny! Anyway, they'll get there. And my mom likes him. Soon, you'll meet her. I mean, if you want to. My parents will love you, Rachael. Well, when you're ready."

"I'd love to meet them. Let's see how we go, anyway."

Spring warmed! Right here, the grass was thick and green after all. Van Cortlandt Park buzzed!

In six weeks, it would be summer!

Chapter 17

"*Another gift*?" Sage drew my gold necklace out of its box. It swirled and flashed.

"He *astounds* me."

"Oh, it's only Bottega Veneta!" Sage threw her head up laughing, and clapped her hands.

"Careful!" I shrieked. Sage clapping the delicate gold made me dizzy.

"What? It's only worth like twelve hundred dollars!" Sage swiped her turquoise spikes, dismissing me. "What's the big deal?"

"Give that back!"

"Aren't you jaded yet? With Peepy's presents?" That was her new name for Harry: Peepy!

"We only met four months ago. So—"

"*It's been four months?*"

"—not yet."

"Do you actually like this thing?" Sage swung the brilliant gold around. Eyed its glinting bean pendant.

I sighed—

"Hang on!" Sage dangled my new necklace in her left hand, squinting at its tiny case in her right. "Uh, you know this is *silver*, right?"

My mouth fell open!

"Hahaha!" Sage's left hand went to her mouth. Her fingernails clattered. My Bottega Veneta necklace waved and twinkled!

"It's gold!"

"Hahaha!" Sage couldn't stop laughing. "Rachael." Her spike underlined some text on its case. "Read it."

"I'm not going to."

"It says so right there."

"It's not like it matters!"

Sage pointed at its case again. "It says: *100% silver*."

"You're teasing."

"I'm not! It says: *Gold-tone necklace from Bottega Veneta*. It says: *100% silver*."

"Fine. Good thing I brought it. It's yours!"

Sage made a face. "Uh, you can keep that." She laid it across my thigh.

We sat on Sage's oatmeal living room carpet. I felt sad. Yet I couldn't help laughing with Sage! Laughing at myself. More than anything else—I felt infinite pity for Harry.

Poor Harry!

"Soon Peepy's gonna buy you a diesel Tesla!"

"He buys lovely things for me."

"Yeah. So uh, how's the drawing going? That three-hundred-dollar Montblanc sketchbook is bringing out your inner Georgia O'Keeffe?"

"It's fine leather. It's lovely." I hesitated. "And—um—the answer is 'No.'"

Sage snorted. "And that English kettle?"

"What about it?"

"That 1757 Sterling Silver makes real good tea?"

"You know I don't drink tea."

But as usual, Sage was right! I decided not to tell her about the Replogle Marin world globe Harry bought me the week before. The one that wouldn't spin.

"How's it going with Adeshina?"

Sage stood. "Why?" Victory curled up in Sage's armchair. Sage slid onto her armrest to stroke my puppy. Victory flicked their russet ears.

"How's it going with him?"

"It's going okay."

"How long have you been dating?"

"A few weeks." Victory yawned under Sage's hand. "I don't know if we're really *dating*. We've met like—I don't know." She gazed lovingly down at Victory. "A few times, I guess."

"How many times have you met?"

"I don't know. Maybe like three times." Now Sage yawned. "I'm not too sure."

"What's he like?"

"I mean, he's cool. He's looking for work. New York isn't good to everyone."

"How old is he?"

"I don't know. In his thirties? He's a *man*, anyway." Sage giggled. "It's good to be seeing someone. But I don't even know if I can call it that. He's a character, that's for sure." Sage stifled another yawn. She pet Victory, who opened and closed their jaws. "He's... I don't know, I guess I like him."

"Really? *You*?"

"Time will tell, anyway."

"I want to know more about him."

"Well—" Sage swooped Victory up. Hugged them into her chest. Sage spoke to Victory, looking into their eyes. Not to me. "—like I said Vicky, Adeshina is a *character*, isn't he? Yes he is. And sometimes he gets real *loud*, doesn't he? He only moved to America not too long ago. He's from Yorubaland, baby Vicky. I haven't visited Africa yet. Neither have you, huh, baby? Neither has Rachael. But my man's from another land." Sage stretched her left spikes to her open window. "Far, far away from here. And he's acclimatizing to the U.S. He wants to start a business. But I think he'll take any job he can get. Come to think of it—" Sage glanced out of her window. "—I don't even know his situation. Like, the terms of his stay, or whatever. I barely know him yet, Vicky. I *barely* know him. What do I like about him? Um, he's hot. He's a *man*. At least he's got *that*." Sage burst out laughing! "People can identify however they like. Animals, too. Forget about a free country, it's a free world! But—at least, I *assume* Adeshina is a man." Sage peered out into the skyscrapers again. Lights illuminated her beautiful face. "But who knows? He presents himself as one. That's all *I* know. I suppose I gotta ask." Sage yawned. "But like, how would I even ask?" Sage swallowed. Blinked. Chuckled. "What do you think, Vicky baby? Is he trans or something? Now your mommy got me thinking about it, yeah, I do kinda like Adeshina. He's beautiful. And he's so funny! Like, he's got this great—this *wild* sense of humor. It's kinda hard to explain it, you'd have to meet him, baby, in order to understand him." For some time, I watched Sage contemplate. At last, she opened her mouth. "But your mommy's not meeting him—*no she's not*—'cause your mommy's dangerous, we all know *that*, don't we, Vicky? She's a tigress in the jungle, Rachael's some kinda way, you know what I'm talking about, Vicky baby? Mommy's a damn huntress when it comes to hotties like Adeshina, like Xavier and half this City, *listen* to me baby! She's a bad girl!" We laughed! We laughed! "Rachael's not to be trusted around hotties of any gender identity, period. She'll eat them right up! I mean—*or* she'll find them and hide them away for later. *I would know,* right? She tried herself on *me*!" Sage's massive, dark eyes gleamed down into mine right now. *In another lifetime.* Infinity tears dripped down my cheeks once again, and Sage saw everything this time! Our laughter erupted. So many feelings—everything all at once—so much eternal beauty. I glimpsed Sage's infinity tears, too! Eye contact! *Oh, in another lifetime, Sage and I, in another lifetime.* But not in this one. Infinity tears splashed everywhere! Fiery laughter burned my throat! "Did she tell you that story, Vicky? Your mommy tried her dirty tricks on me, too! She'll try her magic on damn near anyone she sees. Rachael's got that witch magick—no, not in a bad way, Vicky—I mean Mommy's a wonderful magical sorceress woman who'll take your heart's one true love—straight out of your arms!" I couldn't believe my ears! "But we love her, don't we, Victory? She knows I'm only joking, of course we love our Rachael. Of course we do. Always. But I'll keep any man clear out of her sightline! Anyone—*anyone Mommy likes*—is gonna fall under her special sway. That's why we gotta keep them boys in this City locked up before Rachael gets all of 'em, too! The gays, the theys, the baes, and everyone else! All of 'em. The *girls*, the *women*. She don't—" Sage cackled! "—she ain't one to discriminate! I told you, she fell in love with me, too. But I only wanted those men, I told Mommy, 'No,' loud and clear! And she didn't even listen at first, I swear, she was a whole lot! But that's all in the past now, and Rachael gave up right after I told her I was looking for a man, and *only* a man—if *anyone* at all, but back then I was happy all on my own. Still am, Vicky! Happily single. Just like Rachael pretends she is!"

"Sage!" My breath heaved out of me. Sage bounced Victory up and down. Victory licked Sage's laughing face. Sage wasn't done!

"But Adeshina's cool, baby, and we only met like twice so far, anyway. He got that thing going on. But I'm cool, we're cool. *You* can meet him, Vicky baby. He's loud sometimes, got this great laugh! I hadn't been on a date in so long. Then I go to this thing, and he's all, 'Oh, what's your name? Where you from?' And he's chatting, and I'm like, 'Whatever.' I don't even like being approached like that. But he asks me out, and in my head I'm just—you know—'Mm, you know what? Why not.' He was cute. Made me laugh within five seconds of meeting me, honestly."

For the first time, I noticed that inner smile. That wonderful glowing smile, inside myself! The one I knew Sage felt when she thought about Xavier and me. And, just the way I couldn't stand the idea of Sage meeting Xavier— *apparently* Sage wouldn't allow me to meet Adeshina. So I contented myself to imagine Sage's gorgeous new person. I exhaled. Her man! Maybe.

"I probably shouldn't give your mom every detail, right Vicky? Ah, whatever! Adeshina said I was beautiful. He took me to dinner, I don't know where he gets his money. I offered to pay, he refused. That was like—a month ago? Less. But he's kind, but I don't even *know* him yet. It's just nice to feel desired. Like there's someone in New York who wants me. Who wants to get to know me. It's a good feeling. He knows how to sweet-talk, is the thing, and it kinda creeps me out a little. 'What you hiding?' I'm thinking! But we're just taking it slow. He'll contact me. It's not like I care, anyway. So many fish in the sea. Especially in the City! We'll see. Who knows, maybe he's the one?"

Chapter 18

The fated day came. Harry asked to meet at eight o'clock on a late spring Wednesday. At his Upper West Side home. He wanted to cook dinner for us in his parlor level. But I had other plans.

I took the 1 Train straight from work. Sweating, I waited on his white steps. Peered up at the white limestone of his tympanum.

His mahogany door opened.

"Come inside."

"Actually, I wanted to tell you something."

"Why are you still wearing that?"

"Work ran late today. I didn't have time to change."

"Really, Rachael?"

I nodded. "I need to tell you something. I'm not coming inside."

"What do you mean?"

"Can we go for a walk?"

"You—" Harry stared at my gray suit. My briefcase on his steps. Reconsidered. "You know what? Fine. Give me a minute."

"Sure."

Harry closed the door. I wondered if I'd ever see him again. I stepped down to the pavement and gazed up through the green foliage. Clouds rolled in, and I wondered if it would rain. In a few minutes, the Upper West Side would be dark.

Had I just seen Harry for the very last time?

Was that it?

Why was he taking so long?

The door clicked. He still wore his dinner suit. And white Golden Goose sneakers.

"So?" A gold eyebrow raised.

"Let's go for a quick walk."

"What's the reason?"

"C'mon." I carried my briefcase under the foliage. Away from the Hudson.

Harry locked his door and jumped down his steps, following like a puppy.

"Please, what's going on?"

"How was your week?"

"My *week*? My week was *busy*, Rachael, and I've made *time* to have *dinner* with you!" Harry huffed and puffed. "You're the *only* thing I make time for! And now—*this*?"

"Yeah. Well, that's good."

"Why are we walking? The salmon is almost ready!"

"I'm not eating it!"

"You're not—" Harry gasped! "—*not eating it*?"

It was overcast. The pavement darkened.

"I'm not coming inside tonight."

"What's the matter with you?"

"Don't you think you're a little obsessed?"

"*Obsessed*!?" Harry choked. "*With*—with *what*!?"

I sighed. "With me. Sage thinks so."

Harry stopped by a tall black gate. "Well, why don't you listen to *Sage* then? What did anything *I* ever had to say mean to *you*, anyway?"

"She's right. Ever since we—you know. You won't stop texting me. You're losing it."

"Golly Rachael, it was just what you *told* me! I couldn't stop thinking about *loving everything*. I'm not *obsessed*. I mean, I do think you're one-of-a-kind. And, you're truly *so special* to me, Rachael. And, yeah, I see a bright future with you, and any home you desire, in any neighborhood, in any city, and several children and grandchildren and—"

"Stop!"

"Rachael—"

"Please." I held up my hand. "Just stop."

I took a deep breath.

I looked into Harry's sky eyes.

"I think we need a break."

Harry gaped.

"Just for a while."

"*It's because of that Chinese man!*"

I was struck dumb.

Harry's gold head nodded up and down. "It's him, I know it, it's him!" His crystalline eyes held mine.

"I've gotta go, Harry." I turned and hurried back to Broadway.

"It's that *Chinese* man!" Harry screamed after me. "You can't hide it! But he's not the man for you! *We love everything*, Rachael! That *Chinese* man doesn't understand loving everything! *I'm the man for you, Rachael*!"

I blocked out Harry's crazed voice.

Within minutes, I ran my briefcase down the steps to the 1 Train. This wasn't even the right train! I tapped my OMNY card and jogged to the end of the crowded platform. I tried not to cry. I just needed to get out of the Upper West Side! I'd take the 1 Train downtown. I sat on the wooden seat. Tears made my makeup bleed now. There was nothing I could do.

"Is everything okay?"

"I'm fine." I tried smiling at the concerned commuter. "Thanks."

"Are you sure?"

"I'm sure. Thank you."

The man returned to his smartphone.

Construction was underway in the station. Yeah—I'd take the 1 Train downtown. At Columbus Circle, I'd get on the D Train.

Destiny wasn't always pretty! The fated train was coming.

Chapter 19

I learned the story from The New York Times.

And from Sage. She told me first.

Apparently, Harry Davis downloaded Tinder as soon as he returned to his empty townhome. The Cajun stuffed salmon he'd cooked for us would never be eaten. He swiped and swiped until he saw her. *Blaise. 32.* They matched, and Harry sent their first message shortly after 8:30 p.m. Who would have guessed he liked Chinese women after all?

I imagine Harry was upset over me. I imagine all he thought of was loving everything. But who really knew? There was no one to suggest one way or another.

Blaise Chung worked for TikTok. As fate would have it, in the ByteDance office—right in the mouth of Times Square! Blaise demanded Harry meet her that night. Nine o'clock in Times Square. Harry agreed.

There is reason to believe Harry caught the 1 Train.

15 minutes after mine!

Downtown!

Rain poured, and two strangers made eye contact in Times Square. I don't know whether they had an umbrella, I don't know what they wore. Yet, beyond all doubt, I know that their eyes locked. Their Tinder messages indicate they met in front of the NYPD station soon after nine o'clock. Rapidly, they were smitten with one another.

I want to know what Blaise Chung was like. Was she as disillusioned as the rest of us? With capitalism? With social media? With the nine-to-five rat race of our City? Of our world? What did Blaise's smile look like in the flesh? What was Blaise's expression when Harry touched her?

I bought an online New York Times subscription just to find out. I Googled Blaise, I stalked her LinkedIn and her Facebook. But the beautiful photographs I found of her gave no answers. At a certain point, I gave up. We could only imagine.

All I knew was that Blaise Chung was no saint. Sage was pretty sure of this, too. I saw it in her eyes. And anyway, would a saint insist on meeting their brand-new Tinder match that quickly?

From Times Square, headed for one home or the other, Blaise and Harry descended once again into the subway. Bodies dashed about down there, and rain leaked through the concrete layering, so that the gray labyrinth that is Times Square–42nd Street station was hazardously wet. Yet Blaise Chung and Harry Davis were enamored with one another. Sage agreed—it was the only explanation. Nothing in their systems. No time for anything other than each other. Each other—and words! And thanks to eyewitnesses on the train platform, we know what they said. Their words became famous:

"I love you." Blaise looked up into Harry's eyes, twinkling like the sky.

"I love everything." Harry gazed down into Blaise's.

"I love everything too." Blaise smiled.

And they swung each other around underground. Rain-soaked commuters dodged and weaved. Several overheard Blaise and Harry chanting now:

"I love everything! I love everything! I love everything!"

Infinite eye contact burned—connecting Blaise Chung and Harry Davis for all eternity! They saw infinity in one another's eyes:

"I love everything! I love everything! I love everything!"

And someone slipped on that yellow plastic, and Blaise and Harry tumbled down onto those filthy tracks, and the fated train arrived!

I saw a photograph in the New York Times.

Inside the train that killed them:

An advertisement for TikTok.

An advertisement for Chase Bank.

An advertisement for Tinder.

Chapter 20

I felt so guilty.

I thought I understood guilt… wow, was I wrong!

Maybe it made me a bad person—but I tried separating myself from what happened. See, there was no way for me to know what *really* happened! What really went through his mind after I left him. *Why* he met Blaise so quickly. *Why* they slipped on that yellow plastic.

Yes, the plastic was wet. But—*why*!?

But there were things I did know. Cold, hard facts. I spoke to the NYPD, I even spoke to Harry's mom. I told you—I bought a New York Times subscription. But it was like someone else did all of that—not me. It was like those things *did themselves*! I can't explain it. I needed to put my body on that traitorous train platform. I *had* to know everything.

And pretty soon, I came to my conclusion:

It was all my fault!

Of course it was! Sage and I had known it for weeks—Harry was head-over-heels in love with me. Absolutely obsessed. I only wanted a break—I never told him, 'Never!' Yet when I left Harry by that tall black gate—and that moment will haunt me forever—I broke Harry's heart, and I made him lose his mind. A question arose in my defense:

'But if he loved you, why would he tell Blaise he loved *her*, less than an hour later?' Two eyewitnesses verified Blaise and Harry's impassioned dialogue. And after all, 'I love everything' was not the type of phrase you heard every day! Who could possibly have invented Blaise and Harry's infamous words?

It all happened! And they said 'I love everything' *because I'd planted that idea in his dangerous mind.*

Blaise Chung and Harry Davis loved everything because I loved everything!

Blaise Chung and Harry Davis died because of me.

Yet even in those darkest moments, I knew in my heart that I would never stop loving everything. And if that made me a terrible person... Well, then I was a terrible person. I just couldn't not love everything.

This meant I loved Harry Davis. Always.

Yes, this meant I loved Blaise Chung. I don't want to tell you how many times I tried to apologize.

This meant I was supposed to love myself, too. I tried!

And with time, I finally looked at things differently. Guilt would shadow me for the rest of my life. Yet my beautiful friends reminded me of certain truths.

Destiny isn't always pretty.

Some things can't be controlled.

The words exchanged between Blaise and Harry were facts.

Yet Harry's state of mind—Blaise's state of mind— were unknowable!

What happened was next-to-definitely an accident.

And I was as close to the ultimate truth as I could ever possibly be.

Devonte helped me realize all of this. Sonya helped me realize all of this. Tiana—my ex—helped me realize all of this. More than anyone else—*ceaselessly*—Sage helped me realize all of this. I rediscovered self-love. And no matter what form it took, I accepted destiny. Without those people, I would never have gotten there.

I've said it before! I am nothing without my friends.

I am lost without Sage Knox!

My older brother was there too.

Even my little old mom!

But Xavier?

Xavier was nowhere to be seen.

Chapter 21

I texted him. I called him. If I'd known his address, that's where I would have gone.

Silence.

"Xavier." I said his name out loud. "What's wrong? Xavier. *Xavier*?"

I had absolutely no idea why!

One day became two. Two days became three.

Three days became a whole week.

A week became two!

His shoots filled my Instagram feed. Over and over again, his beauty took my breath from my lungs. I saw everything. As far as I saw, his life continued as normal. Yet after Thursday May 30th, 2024, I just didn't hear from him. I didn't even get his read receipts. Nothing.

I couldn't make sense of it! Was it something I'd said? Had I made some wrong move? Yet again: *all my fault*. As usual, I'd been way too much. Way too fast. Over-the-top with all my feelings. Feelings that just weren't reciprocated! The situation was comparable to Harry's. With Harry, I'd decided I needed a break. Evidently, Xavier had decided the same! Evidently, he'd decided to ghost me.

I'm telling you: those last weeks of spring were not my best.

So I went to Sage's place!

"Trust me. Rachael, trust me! It's all gonna be okay. Remember when I lost Wei Yong? That whole time was one of the worst of my life. I was in the trenches. Just the *worst*. Me and my whole family. You remember, right? That whole time was so tough. *Unimaginably* tough. And what did you say to me? You said, 'I love you.' You told me, 'I'm gonna hold your hand, and I'm right here with you.' You said, 'Always.' You said, 'Everything is gonna be okay, Sage.' You remember, right? And I thought you were crazy. It made no sense. Why should he go? How could it possibly be justified? I thought there was no life without my cousin. I know you remember. And you know what, Rachael? The way it turned out: *You were right*! But *at that time*!, I could have sworn you were wrong. How could everything work out? But it did. Because it always does. It's all going to be okay. Think about how many times you've told me that. *I* know this—and *you* know this. Right now, there's way too much going on. Right now baby girl, you're in the trench. Peepy is gone. Peepy's rebound girl is gone. You had nothing to do with that, *nothing* to do with that, but if you wanna believe they're dead 'cause of you, have at it. Be my guest, you know what I'm saying? You're gonna get over this, Rachael. It's gonna take you time, but you've gotta let it go. You're *gonna* let it go. All of it. You want to believe it's all your fault? Everything? Really? Nah, girl, you've gotta move on. It's gonna take you time." Sage closed her eyes. "I mean, you think about Acacia, right? 12 years is nothing, I still think about her every day. But *at that time*. Do you remember how hard that was for me? And you told me, 'I've got you, and I love you, and everything is gonna be okay.' And it's like with Wei Yong! I told you, 'No, Rachael, life is never gonna go back to normal. Never. Acacia is *way* too young. *There is no justification*. There are no answers. And like, there *is no normal* without Acacia. Don't you dare say that, not even for one second!' You didn't know Acacia the way I knew her. Okay, you say you loved her, but it's *different*, right? Do you have any idea how much I miss Acacia? *Any idea* at all? Like, *every day*? And it was all of us, and I mean, *that* didn't change you, you're always going to shine just like the sun, Rachael, nothing's ever going to change you. Not Peepy, not anyone! Nothing's ever going to wipe that smile off your face, you have to believe me. But like I said, if you wanna go on crying, be my guest. Only *you* can make this change. The only one that can let it go is gonna be you."

"But then there's the whole—" speaking through tears was impossible! "—other thing."

"I know, baby girl, but Xavier's going to come to his senses soon. Like I said, right now, there's way too much going on. You're in the trench! This is the toughest time of your life, but you know what? Life is hard! It's gonna kick you down, but you're gonna get right back up again. It's life, girl! And you've gotta be strong. Now is your time, Rachael, because this is the time that's gonna teach you so many lessons. And you're gonna evolve. You're gonna bloom! You're gonna metamorphose and on the other side you'll spread your wings. What can I say, I mean, we're such different people. You understand that. You're never gonna know the type of hardship I've known. We agree on that. But look at me? I'm pretty good, right? Just think about what I've been through. All of it. The scarcity. The racism. Losing multiple friends and family members before I even got to finish high school. And you know I was an okay kid, I mean, before you met me, you don't know every detail, but you know I was basically okay. Nothing was ever easy. But you know I was alright. My point is—I learned to be strong. I mean, seven years old. Your situation is completely different. We're so different, right? We're always going to be different. But yeah, I think you're learning *now* what I learned *as a kid*. It's different! But you're just learning that resilience. No one's gonna teach it to you. You learn it all on your own. But what am I even saying? Guilt is one thing. But that's not food insecurity for part of your childhood. Rachael! You're *fine*, I mean, c'mon. What are we even talking about?"

"It's not comparable."

"You're gonna be *fine*."

"I'm gonna be okay. But Xavier."

"Give him time. And if not, like I said—*resilience*. But I just know, Rachael." Sage shrugged, palms to her ceiling. "I just know. He needs time. For now—I mean, he has his reasons. It happens. I could be wrong, maybe you'll never see him again. He has his reasons. I've lost count of how many people have gone and ghosted me. You just get over it, it's normal. You stop caring. If I'm wrong—if Xavier's gone for good—you learn that..." Sage sighed. "...that strength. That resilience. You've just gotta be strong. You get over Xavier. You move on. Same thing, Rachael! You let it go. But I'm *telling* you. He has his reasons. Someone takes some time to think—it doesn't mean they ain't coming back. It's not an accident. But, here's the thing. Something happened, and he decided he needs time. But you *will* hear from him. I know because I know. And because I know you. And because you met him between 3:30 p.m. and 5:10 p.m. And just *because*, girl."

"It was *after* that time window, I told you! *We're talking about two weeks.* As of today, it's been *two weeks* I haven't heard from him. Not one read receipt. I wanna believe you, but you literally haven't even met him."

"I know star-crossed lovers when I see them!"

"Okay, but Xavier is a certain way. It's like, Xavier's *over there*. I'm *over here*. He's always been like that. I always knew this was going to happen. He keeps his distance, he always has.”

“Okay, so he keeps a distance!”

“But—”

“But nothing! You *get over it*. I mean, you *get over* what happened with Blaise and Peeps. It’s not your fault.”

“It’s my fault.”

“It’s *not your fault*. Rachael, it’s not your fault.”

Tears and tears.

“It’s not your fault. Forget about Peepy.”

“Don’t call him that!”

“Forget about *him*. Both of ‘em. Any man! You come first. Xavier comes second. Peeps ain’t coming back.”

“Harry!”

“*There is no Harry*. Peepy is gone.”

“Xavier is gone!”

Sage looked through the waterfall of my eyes. “Xavier.” Radiance in Sage’s eyes. “Is.” Eye contact. “Not.” Sage couldn’t have been surer. “Gone.” Sage smiled.

But Sage was wrong. It was two weeks of silence. The worst part was that I *was* over Blaise and Harry. For now, that was done. I was as close as I’d get to forgiving myself. I was as close as I’d get to loving myself once again. The worst part was that all I thought of was Xavier! I’d texted him far too much—about everything except the train—

about Sage, about Isabel, about Tiana, about Victory, about my lunch, about loving everything, about me, about work, about my coffee, about my bracelets, about my parents, about my lonely little life, about *him*, about how much I missed him, about how lost I felt without him. Why was he gone now, when I needed him most? I thought I'd found the solution to the meaninglessness of modern life. I thought I'd found the answer to the capitalism problem. I'd thought it was love! But Sage was wrong. Xavier wasn't coming back.

"Give him time." Sage smiled into my eyes.

"He's not coming back."

"I'm done with you." Even Sage abandoned me now! "I'm done talking about you. I was in Harlem, right. I got my braids done at this place. I mean, I don't go out, I just got my braids done in East Harlem. Well, not *East* Harlem, this place near, uh, Marcus Garvey Park. I know you don't go to Harlem. I just wanted to get my hair braided. But this white person comes in, she's got like something going on with her eyes. I don't know if that was *glitter* or like some kinda silver eye shadow, but it's all messed up. She dumps her things down in the first booth, it's like this giant black suitcase, she's got a whole trolley, right? And she's talking about the sun, she's complaining about the heat, she's talking to herself, right? I can hear what she's saying. And *then*—she goes up to the stylist, demands free extensions.

Everyone's like, 'Say what?' And this girl—she looks like someone's grandma, I should say Momma at least, she ain't a girl—this woman's asking for free extensions. She wants the gold ones. But she wants them for free. At first, the staff are waiting for her to leave. People are getting their locs done, they're trying to mind their own business. And then this one thick stylist, she starts talking to her. And I know what's going on, this woman's trying to hustle, she's got something she's trying to trade, right? And she just wants those damn extensions. But I know it's not gonna work. I'm not even from Harlem, right, but I can tell this ain't what happens in here, there's a time and a place, but maybe I'm wrong right? I've been here before but I've never seen this woman before. I'm familiar with this establishment. She's disrupting. She's gotta go! Everyone wants this woman to leave—this silver eyes. But this one stylist is talking to her, and maybe I'm wrong, you know? I can see what silver eyes is trying to do, but you know, maybe I'm better off just trying to close my eyes and resuming my conversation with my stylist. I'm not from this neighborhood, but I *swear* this woman ain't either, I'm not the only one in the room who feels it. And they're yelling, this big stylist and this silver eyes woman, and I swear it's about to pop off, everyone else is trying to get pampered. Me included. This thick stylist's friend is yelling too. It ain't pretty. And I just wanna get my braids and walk outta that place, I'm starting to get a headache. But the lady in my mirror is laughing and smiling with her hairdresser, and maybe I misread, right? After all, I'm the only Asian, the only Chinese person in the room. Maybe silver eyes is known here, maybe this is just what she does, hustling and yelling and demanding her way. And I can tell something's right about to happen, but now it's simmering down, and I don't know why but my stylist is grinning too. And someone's clapping their hands and the thick stylist's friend is *screaming*, but *then* I can *feel* this Harlem salon lightening up and the woman's things are coming out of her bag in the first booth, she's got like, clips and dyes and *masks* and pads and like—corn chips, it's all there, and like this"—Sage cupped her face with her palms—"my face is in my hands, I'm just hoping this moment is over, but then thick stylist is laughing too!"

We laughed. "What happened?"

"I mean, it just kept *going*, and one moment I think silver eyes is about to leave, and the next moment I think we got a problem! But I've got no problem, you know, I just got a headache at this point. And yeah, there's nothing funny about it, but everyone is laughing, I'm laughing, but the stylist's friend is *not laughing*, she's getting crazy with her hands. But, um, silver eyes left. You know what, I think she did it. Might have. I think she got her gold extensions for leaving something, I don't know what but it wasn't money, or maybe they just gave 'em to her for free. Just like she wanted. Her things were flying out her bag, her *clips* and her *plastic bags* and her *corn chips* and her I don't know *what*, they probably got something! I don't know. Think she got her extensions though! Yeah, she was outta there, good riddance, but for some reason the room is lighter *way* before she leaves, you know what I'm saying? Everyone is laughing in here, except for silver eyes and thick stylist's friend and maybe some others. It's air-conditioned in here, it's sunny out the window. People are getting ready for honeymoons and conferences and kids' birthday parties. I want braids just *because*. And for no reason"—Sage pointed behind her—"*stylist* is laughing, *I'm* laughing, *big stylist* is laughing, everyone!"

Chapter 22

Sage was right. Xavier was silent on Friday. Xavier was silent on Saturday. Xavier was silent on Sunday, and on Monday, and on Tuesday.

But Xavier texted me on Wednesday:

"hey how are you? sorry, ive been busy"

And that was it.

Immediately I texted, five times:

"Xavier? Are you okay?"

"You've 'been busy'?"

"Are you kidding me?"

"What happened? Is everything okay?"

"I miss you"

No reply.

Until Thursday:

"i miss you"

I immediately I texted:

"I miss you too"

On Friday:

"youre busy tonight?"

This time, I made him wait.

I replied:

"No."

"you dont have plans?"

I made him wait:

"*Not tonight?*"

Immediately:

"*dinner?*"

Xavier was a child. Furious, I typed:

"*Xavier, did you see my missed calls? It's been three weeks!!! Why were you silent? Dude what the hell is wrong with you? Did you read a single one of my messages? You're asking me to dinner? No explanation? How*"

I stopped typing.

Closed my eyes.

Breathed.

Opened my eyes.

Totally re-worded the message:

"*Ok*"

Immediately:

"*sarges?*"

I laughed darkly. Xavier knew that was my favorite Jewish Deli.

Home after seven o'clock, I replied:

"*Ok*"

"*great on my way*"

I couldn't believe him!

"*Ok, but my dude, you better have the best explanation of all time. I cannot believe you.*"

I arrived at Sarge's Delicatessen & Diner close to 8:30 p.m. If Xavier couldn't find me—it was his loss, and I was better off without him.

Xavier sat in a booth not far from the entrance, watching me with those eyes. I pretended not to notice his red Falconeri cashmere turtleneck. His black Sea-Gull crystal wristwatch. His wax-styled hair, perfect yet blasé. I looked away from Xavier, pretending to scan the tables at the back of the room.

"Rachael."

I pretended not to hear!

"Are you going to sit?"

I scanned the decorated walls of the diner.

I sat in Xavier's booth, and stared down at the table.

"Hi, Rachael."

Internally, I acknowledged him.

"Ah, hello?"

Somebody—me?—nodded.

"Are you going to say 'Hi?'"

I studied the menu.

Fine. "Hi."

"How are you?"

Okay.

Eye contact.

"I'm okay."

Xavier nodded. "Thanks for coming."

I giggled. "I'm late."

"You're not too late."

"How long have you sat here?"

"I would have sat all night."

"Great. But how long?"

Xavier thought. "Maybe... 45 minutes?"

I shrugged. "I'm gonna get the French onion soup."

"You're not hungry?"

"No, I'm not really hungry. Are those Chinese characters?" I poked his wristwatch.

Xavier laughed. "Ah, some. Some of them are Chinese numerals. Some of them—like this one—" he indicated '4' "—and this one—" he indicated '5' "—they're not Chinese. Although they're similar. They could be Han Dynasty numerals, I'm not too sure."

"So, they're *Chinese characters*?"

Affably, Xavier shook his head. "Some of them aren't modern-day Chinese numerals. Maybe they're Han Dynasty numerals."

"But, isn't there like, Simplified and Traditional—"

"Yes." Xavier smiled. "But these aren't those."

I scowled.

I was friendly with the waitress, though, and broke my smile out just for her.

"Hi Terry! Good, how are you? I'll do the French onion soup, please."

Shaking his head, almost laughing, Xavier ordered.

The waitress went off.

"So how've you been, Rachael?"

I death-stared his infinitely gorgeous eyes.

Xavier saw I wouldn't answer. He nodded.

"Not great, then?"

I wouldn't do it, I wouldn't! I pursed my lips firmly shut and looked away from his eyes so that I wouldn't cry. Staring at someone's black-and-white portrait on the opposite wall, feeling tears come on, I shuddered, and took a deep breath. Though some part of me feared he wouldn't make one, I waited for Xavier's apology, and my fists clenched.

"I got your message. About Victory's new food." He watched me watch the wall.

I wouldn't open my lips. I couldn't—who *knew* what might happen if I did?

He sat and waited for me to speak. But I wouldn't. "So, what else have you been up to? Since I last saw you?"

I just couldn't believe this! My Instagram message about the Royal Canin kibbles I'd bought for Victory—was that the *only* message he'd read from me in *three weeks*?

"I mean if you're not going to talk, I'll talk." Xavier still tried forcing eye contact with me. That was the way it felt, at least.

I wouldn't look at Xavier's eyes, and I would not speak to him. First, I needed him to apologize! But right now, Xavier did *not* read my mind. In moments like these, when I *needed* him to read my mind, yet he *didn't*, or *couldn't*—when he was *oblivious* to my very best efforts to telepathize with him like this—*that* made me more frustrated than he could possibly imagine.

"I'm gonna start by thanking you for meeting me here. I know it was short notice. But I just had to meet you. It's been too long. A lot has happened." Xavier winced. "Since I last saw you, things have changed. Things have been a little tough..."

I listened to Xavier's melodic voice. His life hadn't looked tough at all—I'd followed every irresistible Instagram Story he'd posted since Thursday May 30th, the last time he'd contacted me, the day he disappeared. I'd liked every three- and four- and five-digit-value Reel—it was all so glamorous! But I still wasn't going to engage him, and *I would not open my mouth*.

"...you know. Some things have happened. They changed things. I've been busy with work as well. My shooting schedule's been tight, but it's normal. But some other things did happen, yeah. And maybe that's why I wasn't so responsive."

There it was. My eyes widened in fury, and now I finally opened my lips:

"Are you going to apologize?"

Fire burned behind my eyes, and I stared dead into his.

There, now Xavier had his eye contact! He looked straight back into my eyes, an eyebrow raised in surprise.

"Apologize? You mean for not checking my phone?"

I raised my arm, and when I tell you I nearly...

"I'm so sorry, Rachael."

My arm froze mid-air.

"I've had so much going on! Listen, everything has changed. I'm sorry I'm not on my phone all the time!" Xavier's shoulders rose and fell as he breathed.

My arm fell. But I said:

"You're sorry you're *not on your phone all the time?*"

"I'm sorry I couldn't get back to you."

"I had to *ask* you to apologize to me!"

"I didn't realize you were waiting for an apology!"

"That's why I was silent just now."

He watched me. "I'm sorry, Rachael."

"Xavier, did you get my missed calls?"

"Yes."

"You ignored them?"

"I didn't ignore them. I would never *ignore* you. I was always going to get back to you."

"And did you read my messages?"

"Yes, Rachael. Every single one."

"Really?"

"Yes. I was always going to reply to you."

Somehow, even before he'd answered those questions, I'd always known that Xavier had received every one of my missed calls over the past three weeks, and that he'd read every one of my messages. I'd always known. *Of course he had.*

"Then why didn't I get any of your read receipts? Like, not a single read receipt, since... since May 30th? That was *more than three weeks ago!*"

"I'm sorry, I turned them off. I needed to deal with my problems just for a second. I'm sorry, Rachael!"

"Does 'Sorry' even count if I asked for the apology?"

"Sorry?"

I laughed darkly. "So nearly three weeks of dead silence. And you couldn't give me a single call. You couldn't like a single Instagram Story I posted. You couldn't send me *one miserable little message!*"

"I'm sorry Rachael. Can I tell you what's been going on?"

"I've got so much to tell you, my dude."

"You mean, things you didn't text about?"

I laughed! "Oh, so many things. It's like you said. Everything has changed." I gasped, surprised at myself!

"Everything has changed."

"Summer started yesterday, first off!"

Xavier smiled.

Chapter 23

Sarge's wouldn't stay open much later into the night, as it wasn't that type of diner. Since Xavier and I had so much to talk about, the question became: where to next?

Don't ask me how! Some things defy explanation—and others are best left unsaid. Life is full of mysteries. But the way our conversation went, we were left with only two options:

My place.

Or his.

"I mean, you're more than welcome to come over, I don't know who's home, but you can totally meet my cat! The apartment's ready for you, it's surprising you haven't already been over. It's usually pretty clean, there might be some cat hair and my roommate's things lying around, but you don't care right?"

Actually, I did care—Xavier had no idea how meticulously I cleaned up after myself. How could he have? I contemplated the fact that on multiple occasions, I had visited Harry... *Harry*... Harry in his multimillion-dollar Upper West Side townhouse—yet that I had to ask myself twice about Xavier's neighborhood, that I had never once been invited to see Xavier's apartment, and that, resolutely, I'd attempted to force myself never to mention even the tiniest detail about my *own* home to Harry *nor* to Xavier, let alone ever—*ever!*—to invite either one of them over. I mean, when it came to withholding from Harry and Xavier certain information about my life, I'd failed. Of course I'd imagined each of them in turn, all alone with me at home. Drinking cold apple juice, eating seeded crackers and olives, playing with Victory, looking out my windows at our City. So maybe the things I'd let slip shouldn't have surprised me, right? I'd told Harry about Victory within 20 minutes of meeting him (remind me again how that happened?). I think at some point, I might have told Harry I lived alone. Nonetheless, I never told Harry which neighborhood I called home. Of course, he'd asked! That had been one of the few things he'd actually made the effort to ask me. Other than that, to be honest Harry had always seemed pretty uninterested in all the tiny details that made up my life—and, yes, I'd noticed this about him straight away. Harry wasn't the type of person to ask questions about the person sitting in front of him, or even to talk with much interest or with any detail about anyone other than himself. Yet Harry *had* asked me where I lived. I never told him, and I never came close to inviting him over. On the other hand, long ago, during one conversation or another with Xavier, the name of my neighborhood had slipped out. He may or may not have remembered it, but I *had* told him. And I knew Xavier's neighborhood, because I worked in the area, and quite a few times, we'd met up either during my lunch break, or straight after I finished for the day. Yet I'd never seen the apartment he shared with another male model, not even from the outside. And if tonight, we really *were* going to continue talking like this—well then, it really *was* his place or mine. Like I said... life is full of mysteries. And for me, the decision was easy.

"Your place is in Tribeca, right?"

"Yeah."

"Let's go to mine. It's closer."

At the counter, my credit card weaved past Xavier's to the machine.

Xavier frowned at me.

"You can just transfer me half." I stepped out into Third Avenue.

"But I feel bad. I really should have been more communicative lately. You should let me pay!"

"We *always* go Dutch, Xavier."

"But why didn't you just ask them about splitting the bill?"

"They don't do that here."

Xavier sighed. He squinted into his phone to make the transfer. "So, how are we getting to your place?"

"Walking! Yay!"

He laughed. "I thought so."

I looked at him.

"You told me where you live."

So, Xavier had remembered after all! From Sarge's, it was a ten-minute walk to my place. All along, Xavier had deduced that I really *had* made him wait for me to arrive. He'd deserved it! But now the mood had totally changed.

My place was on the fourth floor. I opened the front door and held it open for Xavier.

"Shoes off, please!"

Xavier snickered. "I would have taken them off anyway." He stepped past me and immediately Victory bounced up his leg cheerfully. "Oh, Victory! Hello!"

"Why's that?" I closed my door, bending to rub Victory like I hadn't done so less than two hours before. Once, Xavier had joined Victory and I on a walk, making this the second time they met. Now Xavier treated Victory like a close companion, and as he bent over, and I kneeled, it was like the three of us were one electrified living being—Xavier's soft black waves, Victory's russet heat in the center, my blond hanging bun! Yay!

"Hello Victory, hi, hello! Oh, I'm Chinese, remember?" Xavier laughed. "We always take our shoes off at the door. At least, *we* do. Oh Victory, you're so cute!"

Suddenly, I felt like Xavier belonged in my home! But I didn't say anything of the sort out loud. Instead, I switched on the air conditioner, then went to my fridge. "Xavier, you want something to drink?"

Xavier still bent over, rubbing Victory's russet coat with both hands, grinning as though he'd never been happier. "Ah, yeah, anything! You are *so* cute Victory!" Well, I thought, Victory *did* have that effect on people.

"You want some apple juice?"

"Yeah, sure!" Xavier laughed.

I can't tell you how happy it made me that he'd agreed. Pouring two glasses, it took me a second to remember that not everyone even *liked* apple juice. What were the odds that Xavier did? I was too curious not to ask the strange question:

"Do you actually *drink* apple juice?"

Xavier stood, smiling. "Yeah?"

"Are you *sure*?"

"Yes, I drink apple juice, why?"

"I was just wondering." Softly, I smiled to myself, returning the Mott's bottle to the fridge. I liked switching up the brands! "Why don't you take a seat?"

"Ah, where should I sit?" Xavier smiled at me sheepishly.

I shrugged. "Wherever you want dude!" I handed him his glass. "I'm just gonna go to the restroom."

"Maybe on the sofa?"

I looked at him. "Um, sure? Just make yourself at home."

Xavier stepped in his white socks over to my sofa. Victory bounced after him. I went into my half-bathroom and locked the door behind me.

On the toilet, it occurred to me that Xavier might feel nervous in my apartment. There were multiple potential reasons for him to feel a certain way, after all! I was still mad at him, although when he'd apologized at Sarge's— even *if* I'd demanded it—I'd started feeling better. About Xavier, about the whole situation. About everything. So, even though I was upset underneath, on the surface I felt some obligation to make him feel at ease. It *was* his first time at my apartment. And who knew, maybe it would be his last? There was no denying it: the thought made me really sad. Either way, I felt I should be hospitable.

Back in my little living room, I went to the kitchen counter to get my glass of apple juice. "Anything else I can get you?" I looked over at Xavier, sitting on the edge of my twilight blue sofa with his back straight. His glass was in his right hand, perched on his right knee, and his other hand rested on his other knee. Xavier peered over his shoulder down at Victory, who lay curled up on the sofa to his left. Xavier looked so... polite! Not uncomfortable. Just... overly polite, and not quite settled.

"No, I'm okay. You have a really nice place, by the way." Carefully, Xavier looked up at me.

My sofa technically had room for three, though three people would have a hard time not being in physical contact with one another. I had an armchair to the left of the sofa, and though the two pieces of furniture didn't belong to a set, it was twilight blue too. In a second, I'd sit in my armchair. But first I wanted to take my socks off!

"Thanks. I'm still mad at you, you know." I stood on my ash carpet, looking down at Xavier with one hand on my hip.

"Yes, I figured. I'll make it up to you."

"I'm not sure how you're gonna do that. But you seem a little nervous. You can feel comfortable here, okay? We're just talking, right?"

"Yeah. Thanks, Rachael." Awkwardly, he sipped his apple juice.

"I'm gonna take my socks off. You can take yours off too if you want. Please, just make yourself at home. *Relax*!" I giggled.

"Yeah, okay." Xavier started peeling off his white socks.

I went to my bedroom to put my socks away. I untied my hair and looked in my mirror. My makeup was smudged and messy, as I hadn't touched it up since that morning before work. But I wasn't making any effort right now—not for *Xavier*. Nonetheless, I picked up my Miss Dior and sprayed my black blouse twice with it. I'd done it absent-mindedly, and immediately I felt annoyed and disappointed with myself! I stood with my hands on my hips, glowering at myself in the mirror.

I closed my bedroom door and stepped barefoot over to my armchair. I looked at Xavier's elegant bare feet as I sat down. Victory separated us.

"Where did you want me to put my socks?" Xavier's white socks dangled in his left hand, hilariously!

"*Oh* my God, wherever you want, man! Are you being serious?" I frowned at him suspiciously.

Xavier laughed. "*Okay*, okay!" He laid his socks on the carpet between us.

"You know you can feel comfortable here, right?"

"I *know*."

"Do you feel nervous or something? Everything okay?"

"Well, you said you're mad at me."

"Okay, but you don't have to act like you don't know me. *I* invited you here, remember?"

"Fine."

We were silent for a little while. I reached over both blue armrests to caress Victory, and Xavier sipped his apple juice. I folded my legs underneath myself, so that my knees pointed toward Victory and Xavier.

"Did you want to tell me something, then?" Xavier gazed at my blank television screen.

"Yeah. I did. But, you were gonna tell me what happened in the last few weeks, right?"

Xavier inhaled. He exhaled. He took a sip of his apple juice. "I'm gonna tell you, yeah. But I was hoping you'd talk first."

"Talk about what? I've already told you everything. Over text, I mean." I rubbed Victory faster. This was untrue—of course Xavier didn't know about Blaise and Harry. About my guilt over the past three weeks. About all the conversations I'd had with all of the closest people in my life. And about how much worse his silence had made it all. His absence. Maybe I shouldn't have—but I felt guilty about the lie I'd just told Xavier. "You didn't even read my texts."

"I *did*, I told you! I read all of them."

"*All* of them? I sent a lot."

"I read everything."

I sighed. "Xavier, I really missed you." I looked in his infinite, beautiful eyes now.

"Me too."

"No, you didn't miss me."

"I promise you, I did."

"Then why didn't you contact me? I'm talking about *one message*!"

"Okay, you're right. I should have been more communicative. Actually, we should have talked more about our relationship from the start. But, if I'm being honest, that's one thing I've always liked about us. That we don't *need* to talk."

Again, I was swept up in that feeling that Xavier knew me, maybe even better than I knew myself. That feeling that Xavier read my mind! "Yes, I feel the same way."

"See? One of the unspoken things in our relationship has always been—*that*."

"That we didn't need to say anything."

"Right."

We looked at each other. Here, again, was this deep sense of connection with Xavier, this telepathic understanding, this destiny thing. It was wonderful.

"But we should still communicate better."

"Yes. You know, that was always a problem in my past relationships. That lack of communication. But there were other issues too." I sighed. "I guess, if you wanted, I could tell you why my last relationship ended."

"Yes. Please do." Xavier watched me with those eyes.

"Well, I don't like talking about it. You know that I don't like talking about him. Ed, that was his name. Now you know. Anyway, I guess the time for being secretive is over." I heaved another sigh. "We broke up because he cheated on me. Like, long-term. There might have been more than one woman. But he cheated on me for about half of the duration of our relationship. And when I found out—" I shook my head. "That's just—that's just the one thing that rubs me the wrong way. You know? Cheating. I can't handle it. And why should I?"

Ever so gently, Xavier cracked his knuckle. "Well, I guess there's one more thing I want to tell you, too." *Oh no*. Really? I watched his curved lips as he spoke. "That was actually the cause of my most recent breakup, too." I stared. "But, you know, the other way around." I shook my head. "I just felt like I should tell you." Xavier closed his mouth.

And that was it. I closed my mouth too. I narrowed my eyes, and nodded at Xavier. "You cheated on Cora." I nodded until Xavier nodded back. And now, we'd reached the point of no return.

"I knew you wouldn't like that," Xavier said sheepishly.

A sharp sting in my knee made me look down. I realized I dug my nail into it. I stood.

"You've gotta go, Xavier."

Chapter 24

It was over. Xavier had already upset me deeply. It didn't matter how many times he apologized for his silence. So when he told me he'd cheated on his ex, I kicked Xavier out of my apartment. I told him I'd call, and I showed him the door. Once I realized Xavier was a cheater, I couldn't stand another second around him.

We agreed to meet one more time. I don't know why—I think the main reason was that I just didn't want to end everything on those terms. We'd always gotten along so well. It didn't sit well with me to kick Xavier out of my apartment and just never see him again. Maybe that logically made sense! But in practice—it did not. On top of this, Xavier still hadn't told me the reason he'd stopped talking to me for nearly three weeks. And part of me knew that I had the right to know.

An entire week passed before we met for the last time—actually, it was eight days. The feeling between us had irreversibly changed. He texted and called, but I only replied about once each day. The day after I kicked Xavier out of my apartment, Xavier texted, and I responded. It was obvious to him I was deeply upset, and it was clear to me that it was over, even if that apparently wasn't what he wanted. I needed to tell him *why* it was over. And I could

only do that in person. I wasn't one to end a relationship—
official or otherwise—over the phone. Plus, like I said, I
actually *wanted* to see him one more time. The truth was
that behind my short texts... all I thought of that week was
Xavier. I couldn't stop. We planned to get ice cream on
Saturday. I know it sounds funny—but ice cream it was.
And after that, I didn't want to see Xavier ever again.

Saturday came, and when Xavier appeared through the
glass door of Chocolate House Astoria, something
happened. Suddenly, I was only happy Xavier was here.
But, of course, I'd anticipated this. So I folded my arms as
Xavier sat across from me. A jewel shone in his ear—but I
banished any positive thoughts toward him from my mind!
I knew that I'd cry today—but to the best of my ability, I
would prevent it. Today would be a warm goodbye, a
cheerful day of reminiscence, and ultimately a happy day!
In my life, every day was.

Xavier told me he wasn't a cheater. He told me that
he'd only ever cheated on his ex, Cora, and never on
anyone else. But to me, one time was one time too many. It
didn't matter if he'd cheated on one woman or on more. It
didn't matter that Cora had cheated on him too! After
today, I would never see him again. For these reasons, I
tried not to question him. Instead, I let myself enjoy the
moment. Here we were, eating ice cream together. And the
feeling between us was positive—we understood one

another. Relentlessly, Xavier told me he wanted to try again.

"As soon as you're ready."

But I told him, 'No.' Flatly and simply. I told him I wanted today to be a happy day, because it was the very last. I smiled through my tears. Xavier cried too, and once, I saw him smile back at me. And I felt it and I saw it and I knew it—the man really did want to be with me. To you, and to anyone other than Xavier and I, the fact that of all moments, *this* was the moment Xavier invited me to his apartment once again—and moreover, that yes, *this* was the first time I accepted—it seems completely absurd, right? I know it. But like I said, we understood each other. I was fully aware that Xavier only wanted to convince me to change my mind about leaving him. And Xavier was fully aware that me going to his apartment was my weird attempt to make our farewell a happy one. Yet mutually, we decided on it.

And now, for the very first time, I was in Xavier's home.

Xavier had lied. His apartment *was* messy.

It was a spacious two-bedroom walk-up in Tribeca. He lived on the third floor, and surprisingly his lovely building didn't have an elevator, which I liked. Nevertheless, the living room was strewn with sporting equipment, expensive clothing, picture frames, and small pieces of furniture. A wooden canoe occupied one wall of the room, and a fine layer of cat-hair lay over the knotted rug.

"I'm assuming your place is unusually messy today?"

Xavier looked at me. "What do you mean?"

I looked back, waiting for him to take the joke. "You're saying your place is always like this?"

He became playful. "You're welcome to clean up!"

"Ha. Not likely." I sat on a jade fabric seat, mentally preparing myself to get covered in cat hair.

But I couldn't deny that Xavier's place was really nice. Behind me, two windows opened out onto the multi-level brick tenements across the street. Two more windows— one of them smaller than the others—faced the apartments directly next door, and flanking these, a vibrant pair of ferns thrived in pots. A flatscreen television sat in front of the seat I'd chosen, and two large frames hung on the walls. Beside the TV was an impressionistic painting of orange koi swimming underwater. The other hung behind me: a framed photograph of a jetty extending into an ocean, shimmering with the colors of the sun setting over it. There was plenty of space to put up the pictures lying around the room. Yet I had the sense Xavier and his housemate had gotten used to keeping all these adornments where they were.

I felt sad. Not only was this the first time I'd come here… it would be the last.

Xavier had a nonchalant way of making me feel comfortable in his home. Yet it worked. He even made smoothies for us, with strawberries, apples, bananas, kiwis, and I think other fruits too. Ruby, Xavier's cat, prowled around the corner from another room. But Xavier's housemate, another male model named Peter, was out for the evening.

The room smelled warm and good. But I didn't tell Xavier this. Instead, we reminisced. Our conversation felt happy and sad at the same time, and the truth is that I didn't want it to end. Eventually, we talked about us.

"We've always had a good relationship."

"But we've never been in a relationship."

This stung. I agreed with what he'd said, yet hearing it from Xavier's mouth caused me more pain than I was prepared for. I came back to myself. "I didn't mean it like that. I *know that*. But what about the—the *unspoken* things between us?"

"There's too much unspoken between us."

"I mean, the unspoken expectations. We both felt them."

"Yeah."

"Well, that's what I'm talking about. You're right, we never made an official agreement. Wow, an *agreement,* what are we talking about, *signing a contract* or something?"

Xavier laughed.

"We never had an official relationship. But it sort of— *felt* like one, didn't it?"

"Yes. It did."

Here it was once again. That wonderful feeling.

But no. Why *now*? It was too late. So, I said:

"You know, I'm still waiting for you to tell me why you stopped talking to me."

Xavier sighed. "Okay. But I'm also waiting for you to tell me something, too." He looked at me. "Okay, I'm gonna tell you right now. Someone in my life passed away."

No. "Oh."

"That's what happened."

"Who?"

"Someone. They died. I was really upset about it. That's why I needed some distance, okay? I'm sorry, Rachael, I'm sorry. Maybe I've got emotional problems or something. But when something bad happens, I go AWOL. I'm sorry, now you know."

Someone in Xavier's life had died! "But who? Why wouldn't you just tell me that?"

"Listen, it was... it was someone."

I closed my eyes. "Who died, Xavier?" Why did I feel so uncomfortable all of a sudden?

"I was hoping you were going to talk first. You said, 'Everything has changed.' When we were at Sarge's."

"Yeah, everything *has* changed." Oh no. Was I about to tell Xavier about Harry? "What, you don't want to tell me who it was?" Why wouldn't he tell me?

"I'll tell you. I told you, I don't have any secrets. Especially not from you. Listen, I really like you Rachael. More than you realize. I *wanted* to talk to you in those weeks, I really did, but I was going through a lot. I'm sorry, okay? It's a coping mechanism, it's what I do sometimes. I guess you had to learn it the hard way, I should have explained myself, I know, but I disappear sometimes, I change my phone settings, it's how I deal with my problems. I'm sorry, I should have texted you. How many times do you want me to apologize?"

"You *ghosted* me!"

"I didn't, because I'm here right now. I was never going to stop talking to you."

"You know that *I* could have stopped talking to *you*, right?"

"Yes, I know it. But I'm so grateful that you didn't. I really like you."

"Listen, I like you too Xavier. But I just don't understand why you couldn't send me *one single message* in three weeks. Who was this person, your mother? Listen, someone in my life died too. I had three of the worst weeks of my life. And *everyone* was there for me, I'm talking Sage, Devonte, Tiana—my ex—my *mom*, I spent all my time *crying every day*, and do you know that you just made it worse? Like, *really, really* worse? I wanted to talk to you, but you were *gone*! That was the *worst* time of my *life*. And you were *not* there for me. I'm never going to forget that, Xavier." I nearly teared up, yet again. But I was not going to cry.

Understanding had deepened Xavier's eyes. "You didn't tell me. I didn't know you lost someone. I'm sorry, Rachael. Why didn't you tell me?"

I felt it. I was about to tell him everything. "Well, you weren't replying!"

"I'm sorry. I think I'm going to stop saying it. You believe that I'm sorry, right?"

"Yes, I believe you. And yes, stop saying it." I took a deep breath. "You didn't even reply about the kibbles I bought Victory!"

Xavier didn't laugh this time. "I was having a hard time too! And guess what—obviously it's because of me—but you weren't there for me, either! I take the blame, I don't mean to make it seem any other way. But you know, I really *did* want you to be there for me, too! I *know exactly* what you're *saying* about me being there for you, or *not* being there for you, because I wanted the same thing. You said you lost someone, right? Well, me too, and it flipped my world upside down! Tell me who you lost, and if you want, I'll tell you."

Was now the moment?

I decided that it was.

"Xavier, there's a reason I didn't tell you. I mean, I texted you about everything in my life *except* for this. And *there's a reason*. But I'm going to tell you." I sipped my smoothie and fought back the tears—I was *not* going to cry tonight. "Alright. So, ever since we met... I—" I closed my eyes and touched my fingers to my forehead. I breathed. I opened my eyes. "I was seeing someone. Okay? And—"

"Me too."

My breath caught. No! No, no, no. *No!*

"She's the one who died."

No. I could not believe my ears.

"Um, *what*?"

"She's the one who died."

"Who?"

"I just told you."

Nothing was real. This couldn't be happening. "You were seeing someone... and she died?"

"Yes."

"What was her name?"

"Who were you seeing?"

"Xavier—"

"Please just tell me."

"Xavier, *he* died! The guy I was seeing! *He's* the one who died!"

Shocked silence.

"How did she die?"

I felt Xavier's eyes. But I could not look back. "She got hit by a train."

Chapter 25

I have never hated anyone. It's just not really who I am. Ever since I was a kid, I loved people. Everyone! I really can't remember anyone from my childhood who actually *gave* me any reason to hate them. Sometimes I wonder if it's sheer luck—do I love everyone because I see the world through permanent rose-colored glasses? Or do I love everyone because, my whole life, owing either to my nature, or to some kind of fluke, I've been blessed with a sort of immunity to acts intended to hurt me? What if I had my mind, but lived someone else's life—then would I be capable of hate? What if, for example, I'd lived Sage's life? I don't want to pretend no one had ever wronged me. I'd been treated unfairly by people I was only ever kind to. I'd been cheated on. People had been mean to me. But taken as a whole, it never seemed like a lot. Maybe this was why I've never hated anyone.

Yet I nearly hated Xavier. To be honest, I shocked myself! I was shocked that I could feel such negative emotions toward somebody so kind, so quiet, and so gentle. Sometimes, I nearly hated *myself* for nearly hating *Xavier*!

He had never cheated on me. Because we were never in a relationship—I'd always made sure of that. In the same way, I had never cheated on him. Yet the fact that Xavier had seen Blaise upset me beyond any rational attempts to make sense of it all. *Yes*, I'd met Harry a week after I met Xavier, and had seen both right up until Harry's death. *Yes*, from what Xavier had so far told me, I'd seen Harry for longer than Xavier had seen Blaise. *Yes*, Xavier and I were never in a committed relationship. And *yes*, this was because I'd ensured it! But my feelings were my feelings! My feelings were legitimate and meaningful. And I felt jealous beyond all words.

All I could think of was Xavier with Blaise. Doing God knew what together! Everything *we* had done together. If I were to guess, some things we had never done together! I felt horrible. I imagined Xavier together with Blaise. Every time I remembered Xavier's smell... Xavier's warmth... how I felt in Xavier's arms... Blaise emerged, enjoying all of it in my place. And I hated Xavier.

Xavier hadn't sought out the details of the train accident the way I had. But he'd read about Harry in the media, and in Xavier's apartment, I'd confirmed: 'Yes. *Him*.' He told me that he'd met Blaise through mutual friends, and that they'd seen each other ever since the day I told him I loved everything. That had been at Katharine Hepburn Garden, right after we protested for Julian Assange. That day at Katharine Hepburn Garden had been the first time Xavier had held me. The first of many. It had always been one of my very favorite memories with him. But now Xavier told me that it was the moment he decided I wasn't for him. Because I'd told him my deepest secret, that I loved everything! I felt betrayed in so many ways. I felt betrayed by the universe, I felt betrayed by Xavier, I felt betrayed by *loving everything* itself. Julian Assange was freed now, yet I was unable to rejoice at the news. That once-golden memory of Katharine Hepburn Garden was forever ruined. And anyway, it was a lie! Xavier had been serious about me *well after* that moment. I mean, c'mon, who was the one talking about introducing their parents? He'd met mine against my will! *In Trader Joe's*! Xavier had *not* decided against pursuing a serious relationship with me ever since I told him I loved everything. If anything, his feelings for me had *grown* since that moment! So really, this was no reason to be upset. I was upset at *Xavier* for his false claim. I was definitely upset Xavier had seen Blaise ever since I told him I loved everything—he told me he'd started seeing Blaise that very week! But I had no reason to feel hurt that Xavier claimed to have a problem with my love of everything. Nevertheless, I *was*.

I was shocked to find that I was as close to hating Xavier as I had ever been to hating my ex! My ex, Edmund, who two years before had kept another woman on the side, for more than half of the time he'd claimed to have been committed to me. When I stopped to think about it, I became fully aware that, clearly, it was Edmund who had committed the greater crime. When it boiled down to it, Xavier had essentially done what I had done. We'd had a casual relationship, and each of us had decided to see other people. Was this really the behavior of a bad person? If Xavier was a bad person, then so was I.

But on top of seeing me at the same time as seeing Blaise, Xavier had cheated on his ex, Cora. He'd told me so. According to him, he'd only ever cheated on Cora, and Cora had done the same thing. But to me, the number of incidences—even of people—was irrelevant. To me, Xavier was a cheater.

And then there was that whole three-week period when Xavier hadn't contacted me. Mostly, that didn't bother me anymore. But, nestled in history, the fact was still there. When I'd told Xavier I'd never forget about that, I meant it.

When I broke it down like this, it stopped making sense. My anger toward Xavier—my fury, my near-hate— seemed to be owed to those three factors. But then I'd compare the situation to that of Edmund. And there was no question—*Edmund* had done me far more wrong.

So why did I feel the urge to egg Xavier's perfect apartment?

Why did I seriously consider stealing Ruby?

Why did I desire so deeply to break into his home at night, sneak into his bedroom, and cut off all his beautiful hair while he slept?

I'm telling you, if I've ever hated anyone, I've hated Xavier Pang.

He contacted me, of course. He texted me every single day, and fairly often, he tried calling me. But this time, it was me who wouldn't answer.

At least he knew why!

Yet the strange thing was that Sage didn't even pretend to support me in this newfound rage of mine. Part of me felt like it was her duty as my best friend to help me brainstorm ways to take out my revenge on Xavier. Wasn't that what we were supposed to do? I went to Sage with a specific purpose in mind. We were supposed to hate on Xavier together. But for some reason, it just didn't work out like that.

Instead, Sage reminded me of how, when I'd been so sure Xavier would never contact me again, ultimately she had been right, and he *had*.

Sage glowed now, and it was easy to see why. She was officially in the blooming era of a brand-new relationship with her Nigerian entrepreneur man, Adeshina. I recognized what was happening, regardless of the fact he'd apparently turned out to be a Taurus. Slowly, they fell in love. And I could tell that what they shared was real.

At some point, to my horror, something dawned on me. And soon, there was just no denying it. It wasn't merely that Sage refused to join me in my vengeful hate—maybe we should call it 'near-hate?'—of Xavier. It was this. Sage essentially believed she saw something I couldn't see. She didn't tell me this. I was left to figure it out all on my own. It was as though Sage thought herself an actual sage— which she wasn't—as though she believed she was on some level of higher understanding. Long ago, Sage had mentally prepared herself for me to entreat her to help me get revenge on Xavier. She'd prepared herself for the horrible way I felt toward him, and toward his silly cat, too. So, when I started telling Sage I wanted to egg Xavier's apartment, she dismissed me with, in effect, a calm, yet empathetic shrug. When I told Sage I hated Xavier, she only laughed. It wasn't that Sage didn't care about my feelings. She did. It was that, as far as she could tell, she saw right through them.

This was my life for several weeks. Xavier's attempts to contact me slowed down. I'd well and truly gotten over Blaise and Harry. It was summer in New York! And I'd already had a romantic offer from a handsome acquaintance. I turned him down. But I told myself I was open to even better offers.

*

One morning in late July, I got a text from Sage.

"*Have you started talking to Xavier yet?*"

I ignored the message.

At home eight hours later, I stared at it once again.

The answer, of course, was 'No.' I hadn't contacted Xavier since that evening in his apartment. Our final day together. That day had been my gift to him.

But still, I chose not to reply to Sage's text. Instead, I thought.

With a jolt, I realized it had been several days since I'd really thought about Xavier. There was no anger left. I just felt relaxed. I was at peace. And Xavier...

Hm.

The fact that Xavier had been with Blaise—well, he was entitled to that, wasn't he? And right now, it only made me want Xavier more. There was a time when I thought I was unable to love one person. I loved *everything*, after all. But eventually, I learned that my love of everything didn't make me immune to jealousy. It also didn't render me incapable of falling in love with one person.

Sitting at home now, for the first time, it all felt even better than destiny.

It all felt like free will!

It was *my choice*.

I thought about Xavier. Xavier was sweet. He was calm. He was gorgeous. He was...

He was Xavier.

No. Not even loving everything could hold me back from loving one person!

It was more like loving that person *even more* than I love everything.

I picked up my iPhone. I couldn't believe myself! My heart beat in my throat!

"Rachael!"

"Xavier."

"How are you?"

"I'm good."

"I'm so happy you called!"

"I wanted to tell you something."

"Yes?"

"I—I love you!"

"...I love you too."

"I—"

"Rachael, can we meet?"

"...Yes! Where?"

"...Times Square."

Chapter 26

I came out into 28th Street, smiling.

I loved New York in summer. The heat warmed me right to my insides, and today, there was a perfect breeze too. I wandered down the pavement, swaying my head side-to-side in joy. I passed Curry in a Hurry, catching the chatter of some of its diners:

"She moved to Europe, didn't she?"

"No, she moved to Wisconsin…"

I crossed Lexington, looking uptown at the long view—I saw the Chrysler Building in the distance. Opposite, I passed the corner store, I passed the barber. Rose Hill had my heart. I passed that large parking garage, and for some reason, I always loved looking into these. The Latino fruitseller waved at me across the road. We knew each other by sight, and I grinned back. But I didn't look him in the eyes! I sauntered across Park Avenue, slowing to stroke my fingertips through the little white petunias in the flowerbed. Underneath my feet, I felt the 6 Train rumble to a stop at 28th Street Station. I looked into the dark depths of the Station's entrance. It was built into the base of the stunning Prism at Park Avenue South apartment complex, which soared over my head. Its glass was extraordinarily shiny, and I shielded my eyes from its white light as I looked up to where the skyscraper almost kissed the sky.

I dipped my hand into my Zara purse and found my shades. I slipped them on. I looked to my right: echoes emanated from another entrance to the Station that extended below the street. I passed under some pretty flower bouquets. Four guys jostled on the street, mostly wearing shorts and button-down shirts. They all stared straight at me. Maybe it was my sunglasses? It felt like they were right about to talk to me. As I walked a little faster, one of them said something—but if it was directed at me, I paid no attention. Then they were behind.

I paused at Madison, watching a group of tourists ride north on Citi Bikes before I crossed. As far as I knew, we didn't actually own those bikes—we just sponsored them.

But I shook my head. I wasn't going to think about work.

I sighed—soon, the ads would come. But I was barely going to look. They didn't matter anymore!

Instead, I turned into Madison. Here were the arched windows of The James. I crossed 29th, taking a left past Liaigre, the furniture store. Here was The Church of the Transfiguration, with its dark, beautiful courtyard. And on the street, young singles, old couples, all enjoying Saturday.

Across Fifth Avenue there was another beautiful church. I walked under some scaffolding. Would there ever come a day when the City would complete construction? I doubted it. Pedestrians walked on the road here, opposite another vast parking garage. Without looking at them, I smiled at all of the African street vendors. And now Broadway neared. I had options. But it didn't matter which route I took, did it? Just like I said, I knew where I was going.

On Broadway, the regular noise of any Midtown street increased. I heard the growl of car engines, the bleat of truck horns. Several languages spoken over one another. Someone blasting hip-hop music from a Bluetooth speaker. Traffic raced down Broadway's narrowness, and my step increased. This was a Saturday evening in the middle of summer, and New York didn't get any busier than this! Somehow, the crowds still surprised me, and I knew today was meant to be. I'd chosen it!

A beautiful dark-skinned woman neared. Wow!, she was tall, and stepped with pride, wearing a sleeveless scarlet blouse and a black box pleat. And I couldn't believe it—she looked straight at me as she neared! It was like she dared me to look back, yet the thought barely crossed my mind. Now I noticed the bushy black hair escaping from behind her back. Yet we never made eye contact. I felt the warm air move as she passed.

She seemed so glitzy, maybe she'd just exited one of the jewelry shops I looked into now. But I was dubious, as this wasn't the area for the type of jewelry I imagined she wore. The name of this shop was Decent. Most were closed, but in another I saw a kaleidoscope of Arabic perfume boxes. Now I saw ostentatious topaz necklaces, I saw gems crafted into shapes I'd never wear. The sort of pieces—had they been more expensive—that once upon a time, Harry might have bought me. I smiled, remembering him.

And now a gorgeous Black man walked my way. Oh no, was he trying to catch my eye too? What was it today? I tried not to pay him any mind. Nonetheless, I noticed his chest-length gold-tipped dreadlocks. I noticed his bulging pectoral muscles and biceps under his ornate shirt. I noticed the gleaming tattoos covering most of his skin that showed. And who wouldn't notice his sheer size? He might have been taller than Harry. Ignoring his gaze, passing him, I marveled at the fact that two of the most attractive human beings I'd ever had the fortune to see had *both* tried to make eye contact with me. I wasn't imagining it. I knew the feeling. I shivered, despite the blazing heat of Broadway today. Unbelievable.

I smiled, I smiled, I smiled!

You already know this. But I looked for infinity. And yes, I knew where I was going to find it.

Laughing, I smelled fruit smoothies, I smelled burgers. The food trucks were out to play—today had to be the biggest day of their weeks. They were here for the tourists, but I knew I wasn't the only New Yorker who occasionally stopped by for a five-minute meal after work. (Usually I liked the Mexican ones. Sometimes I liked the ice cream trucks!) Still laughing, I gave 40 dollars to a homeless man on the pavement. He thanked me, and I smiled before crossing West 32nd Street. Greeley Square Park was always so cute. You might see a choir sing here, or maybe a wild bouncing castle! Today, there were countless potted plants, patterned street barricades, variously-colored metal chairs, and every type of person. And yes, at the top, ping-pong tables and sweating players!

Koreatown was only really two blocks on my right, and I'd nearly passed it already. I might have been sad, but I was in a sort of state. I'll describe it like this: I wanted time to slow down, yet I also wanted time to speed up. I still had a way to go. I wanted to sprint, yet I wanted to stop! It all happened right now. Everything was here, right here! It was all so much. It was all so...

Perfect!

And yes, I sped up now. I could only go onward! People watched me, not only all the street vendors. I felt it. I knew it. They were not robots, they were real! Yet I looked back at nobody. The colored street barricades were behind me, the people of the tiny Park were behind me. I couldn't help it, I stepped up and over one of those stone blockades lining the street! Koreatown was behind me, and for a block, Sixth Avenue and Broadway sort of became one and the same, almost like a Times Square appetizer. *Yum*!

I barely looked at H&M's giant curving glass to my left. I thought of one thing, and one thing only. I powerwalked up baby Times Square, running left across it before anything could hit me, savoring all of this so much that I just *had* to slow down into Herald Square, Herald Square dancing with its variegated flowers, chairs, shopfront screens, and human beings, all sparkling under the summer green of maples and pyrus trees. I wasn't sure whose statue towered in Herald Square's heart, it wasn't so important to me.

But no, there was no stopping me—not now. I speed-walked past some of the bigger names, which flew up more and more the closer you got to Times Square. Macy's. Santander, who I refused to think about right now. FedEx. You have to understand my love-hate relationship with it all. With capitalism. All I knew was that these things no longer seemed to bother me.

Because!—I'd found the solution.

A plume of steam rising from its sewer hole. Waving flags. A long blue Citi Bike rack, offering just a handful for the taking. Large potted plants whose light leaves flowed onto the concrete, whose dark leaves stood taller. Good old

Dunkin' Donuts—or, technically, Dunkin'. 37ᵗʰ Street, and my heart stopped, because now I saw the lights.

A white family with a stroller, watching me. I swear to you I'm not making this up! It was the amazing shades on my flushed face, it had to be. A teenage couple, the boy with bedraggled long hair under a Dodgers cap, apparently dumbfounded. An aged Latino woman with a walking stick, looking straight up at me! I shook my head, laughing. I loved being looked at.

A Chinese art installation—dozens of hanging lanterns celebrating a new start, and new hope! The block bent ever so slightly to the right. There were more than just plants in pots now, whole trees sprouted from them too. More people! More little chairs! More of everything!

I saw Times Square!

I couldn't believe it, I couldn't believe it. The time was now, and there was no going back. This place had to have a name, I just didn't know it. Any other day, I'd have stopped to learn all about it. Xavier was right—I was very intelligent. Oh—hang on! This was Golda Meir Square, if I wasn't wrong! One of very few statues of women in the whole City, although I knew that soon, about four more would be erected across the boroughs. Yes, she was here, but I didn't check for her statue. I re-directed my attention at the huge black metal sculpture looming over my left. It was terrifying yet beautiful, and I didn't want to know what it meant. I crossed 40th Street. More street vendors, offering sunglasses, framed pictures, hats. A pizza place across Broadway.

And now, televisions and billboards. Champs Sports. "MAKE AN IMPACT." YouTube and TikTok and Instagram logos. More scaffolding and works-in-progress. Darting in-and-out between tourists! And maybe some New Yorkers too. Times Square Tower, refracting the setting sun, opposite Broadway. And opposite 42nd Street, the gleaming H&M store with its entrance under enormous screens, the exact one I told you about, only it was now one big olive-green construction site. This was the power of time.

Yet now we knew how to stop time, didn't we?

The construction walkway was completely packed, and was dark too. It was finally time to remove my sunglasses! Beyond perfect. A huge fluorescent American flag, making me sigh. My heart beating faster. My steps catching. My breath nearly gone.

I ran, I tell you, I ran! Times Square stopped to watch in awe. It overflowed with people—it was so hard to move, let alone run! Yet I ran, and I promise you, no one was unhappy to let me through! This was New York, and this was almost impossible. But so was life itself.

I slipped between everyone. They all wanted eye contact. I loved them!, I loved them!, but my eye contact was special! I span. I sprinted. I sang! Surrounded by pedicabs, demonstrations, LED spectaculars, and jumbotrons, I sang an off-key tune of my own. I was in Times Square, my very favorite place, and the time was right now.

Company, ad, corporation. Look at me, look at me, look at me! Oh, dear God, I saw the red steps!

There were *so many* people! Where was he?

Astoundingly, I sprinted diagonally in between cars! "Woah, Rachael!" I whispered. Oh shoot, several honked! I sprinted faster!

A bonnet touched my leg—shoot, was I alive?

It all ended in less than the time it takes to blink!

Oh!—

Time stopped.

Purer than infinity!

His eyes in Father Duffy Square. No sound. No movement.

All was still, and his eyes were the most beautiful eyes I had ever seen.

Eye contact!

Leaping! On to Xavier! Xavier nearly toppling backwards, yet catching me, Xavier embracing me. My legs wrapped around his hips, my arms squeezing him tighter, tighter, tighter. So sweaty. Tighter!

Movement now—Sound. Ovation. We were in between the two bronze statues, me facing north, Xavier south, and dozens of people, people I would never know, yet *everyone I knew*, cheering! I swear to God, it happened! Tears. Infinite laughter. Hugging tighter. Xavier swaying me gently from side to side. He'd never carried me, yet of course he was strong enough for this. It was easy for Xavier. It was so hot, and it was hilarious. And in his arms I knew all these things:

This was the beginning of everything.

Our future was brighter than the sun.

Our love transcended time.

Our love was stronger than time.

We were stronger than time.

My hands on his strong shoulders, I leaned back to look at him. He still held my entire body. Our eye contact was more than infinity, it was better than everything. Tears shimmered across Xavier's cheeks, and I felt my face was even wetter. Eye contact! We cried, and did the only thing left to do!:

"Hahahahaha!"

Did you enjoy this book?

Follow Cameron Liang on social
media & write your review on
Goodreads and Amazon

<3